FETISHISM

Fetishism

PENETRATE, UTILISE & BOND

Chavanese Wint

Icons Media Publishing

ICONS MEDIA PUBLISHING

Contents

DEDICATION
Shermaine Campbell

If you create the game,
then you create the rules.

Russian Roulette

I'll tease and tempt with each caress,
Playing Russian roulette, no time to guess.

~

With curves that kill and hair so dark,
We'll make sweet music, ignite a spark.

~

Hotel or home, it's all up to you,
As long as my hands can explore your body anew.

~

No disrespect, just pure desire,
You and me, set the night on fire.

~

Forget all else, let's lose our minds,
As I devour you like an omelette divine.

~

You'll never forget this passionate night,
For in each other's arms, we reach new heights.

One

Luna

Click, the room fell silent as I flinched in disbelief, my heart pounding in my chest. A wave of fear washed over me, making my shoulders tense and my breath shallow. The atmosphere was thick with tension, each second stretching out like an eternity. I desperately tried to maintain a façade of bravery, but deep down, I knew I was just a trembling mess. His gaze pierced through me, devoid of any warmth or empathy. It was as if he saw right through my act, exposing the vulnerability I tried so hard to hide. In that moment, the air felt heavy with anticipation, as if something explosive was about to happen.

"You're not going to do it, are you? You're a pussy," I smiled as I taunted him. His eyes glinted with a mix of defiance and desire.

"Is that what you think? You think I'm a pussy?" he chuckled, his fingers gripping the gun firmly.

With a daring grin, he pushed it a little deeper into my wetness, eliciting an involuntary gasp from me. The sensation was intense, sending shivers of pleasure through my body.

"Hmm, that feels so good," I moaned, my voice dripping with anticipation.

He withdrew the gun from my throbbing core, allowing my juices to coat the sleek metal. My breath hitched as he leaned in close, his voice low and husky.

"Okay baby, here's what we're going to do," he whispered seductively, outlining his plan with a devilish gleam in his eyes.

He picked up his beer from the bottom of the bed, taking a long sip and savouring the bitter taste. With a confident stride, he walked over to the window, where he had strategically placed his coke earlier. He carefully lined up the powdery substance on the windowsill. Taking a deep breath, he indulged in a quick snort, feeling the rush coursing through his veins. As he tilted his head back, he relished in the sensation, knowing that every last bit of the coke was now inside him, powering his thoughts and desires. With a newfound clarity, he began to speak articulately, expressing his innermost thoughts with an irresistible magnetism.

"Okay baby, here's what we are going to do," he whispered, his voice dripping with seductive confidence. "We're going to play a little game of Russian roulette, but with a twist."

My heart quickened as I listened intently, hanging onto his every word. He continued, the room filled with an electrifying tension.

"I want you to express your love for me in ways that will leave no doubt in my mind." His eyes locked onto mine, a mix of desire and danger swirling within them.

I couldn't help but feel a surge of excitement mixed with apprehension. This was uncharted territory, a thrilling blend of pleasure and risk.

"But what if I'm not convincing enough?" I asked, my voice tinged with uncertainty.

A sly grin spread across his face as he approached me slowly, the blunt still smouldering between his fingers.

"Oh baby," he purred, his words laced with raw intensity. "If I even suspect for a moment that you're not being completely truthful about your love for me... well, let's just say things might take a very interesting turn."

For your information, I was panic-stricken. The fear coursing through my veins was so intense that I even felt a little pee being released from my vagina as he threatened to shoot my vulva. In that moment, I was scared out of my mind. The loss of control and autonomy consumed me completely. Thoughts raced through my head, questioning what the fuck I was doing. You see, I've always been a very freaky kind of person, but this situation took things to a whole new level. It all started when I was seventeen years old, when I met this older man at my previous workplace. He was a colleague who eventually took me on a few dates. As we got to know each other better, I began to understand his inner demons and the darkness that lurked within him.

He was into BDSM, Bondage, Discipline, Dominance and Submission, which is a variety of erotic practices involving dominance and submission, role-playing, restraint, and other interpersonal dynamics. He taught me a lot about the world of sexual exploration and power dynamics. But after seven years of being together, he unexpectedly ended our relationship. He confessed that I had become too experienced for him and that he desired someone more submissive, someone who would surrender completely to his desires. As our time together progressed, my own dominant side had started to emerge more prominently, which no longer excited him. Despite the end of our relationship, I will always cherish the knowledge and growth I gained from our shared experiences in BDSM. What began as mere experimentation blossomed into a deep fascination and passion for exploring the boundaries of pleasure and pain.

Now here I was, sitting in a hotel room, intoxicated on a cocktail of drugs, completely wasted and ready to indulge in the most intense sexual experience of my life. This was my breaking point, the moment when I realized that my desires, fantasies, and hedonistic lifestyle had spiralled out of control. But despite knowing the risks involved, I couldn't resist the exhilaration of being penetrated by a gun. It was a perverse game that pushed me to the edge, but if I survived this encounter, I vowed to share my story with the world. I knew it was a dangerously thrilling game to partake in, but I'll be damned if I didn't admit how exhilarating it felt. Every nerve in my body tingled as he made his way towards me, holding the revolver high in his right hand. The six chambers glistened under the dim light, and my heart raced as he emptied them one by one before loading just a single round back in. My breath hitched as he spun the cylinder, his eyes locked on mine. With a sudden jolt of terror, he aimed the barrel at me and pulled the trigger. Time seemed to slow down as I squeezed my eyes shut, preparing for the worst. Yet, all that followed was a deafening click. The pistol remained silent, leaving me both relieved and electrified with this dangerous game we had dared to play.

He once again spun the cylinder, pointing it at me with a sinister grin. The tension in the room was palpable as I braced myself for what would come next. Click. Once again, the gun failed to fire, adding to the suspense that hung heavy in the air. He closed the remaining distance between us, positioning himself below me, his gaze fixed on my vagina. With each movement of the gun towards my pussy, I could feel a mixture of fear and arousal coursing through my veins. The feeling was almost unbearable as he slowly inserted the cold metal into my wetness, a shiver running down my spine. With deliberate precision, he began to manipulate the gun inside me, rotating it first to the left and then gradually to the right, intensifying the sensations that pulsed through my body.

My moans grew louder with each passing moment, a testament to the pleasure coursing through my veins. It wasn't the size or shape of the pistol that excited me, but rather the exhilarating knowledge that it was buried deep inside me, a forbidden thrill that made my heart race. The mixture of drugs and alcohol in my system only intensified the experience, leaving me dizzy and consumed by a euphoric haze. This was more than I had ever imagined, surpassing even my wildest fantasies. With a mischievous grin, he repeated the ritual once more, keeping the gun fixed in its position. Locking eyes with me, he spun the cylinder and plucked another cigarette from the ground. As he pulled the trigger again, adrenaline surged through my body, only to be met with the same result - silence from the gun's deadly potential. The tension in the hotel room grew, at this point I think we both knew that we were playing a very dangerous game. As he took another drag of his cigarette, the thick smoke filled the air, adding to the already intense atmosphere. His eyes locked with mine, a mix of desire and control burning behind them. And then, in a bold move, he placed the cigarette between my trembling lips, letting me taste the bitterness on my tongue. It was a subtle act of dominance that sent shivers down my spine and ignited a fiery need within me.

With each puff and exhale, I felt myself surrendering more to his power. Without breaking eye contact, he leaned forward and traced his lips along my jawline, leaving a trail of electrifying kisses in his wake. His hands explored every curve and crevice of my body, knowing exactly how to make me quiver. I could feel myself melting under his touch as he competently teased and pleased me with every caress. Lost in the pleasure he was giving me, I couldn't help but moan softly as his mouth descended upon my most sensitive spot; his expert tongue tracing patterns of ecstasy against my flesh. And when he finally set the gun aside, his attention turned to my throbbing core, devouring it like a man possessed. With every lick and nibble, he took me to new heights of ecstasy, his expertise evident in every motion. It was pure bliss as he devoured me with an insatiable hunger, each flick and swirl sending shockwaves through my body. In that moment, there was nothing else but the intoxicating dance between pleasure and pain that only he knew how to orchestrate so perfectly.

He then skilfully teased my clitoris with his nimble fingers, sending waves of pleasure through my body. In a tantalizing move, he slowly inserted his middle finger inside my wetness, gradually increasing the intensity of our connection. As I gasped with pleasure, he expertly added a second finger, stretching me deliciously. The sensation intensified as his fingers explored deeper, hitting all the right spots. With every movement, he alternated between sucking on my sensitive clit and thrusting his fingers inside me, pushing me closer to the edge of ecstasy. In that moment, I surrendered completely to the sensations, losing myself in the blissful dance between heaven and hell. As he continues to create masterpieces with his skilled tongue, my eyes drifted towards the ground where a revolve lay. Mesmerized by the intricate patterns of his oral artistry, I couldn't help but feel a surge of desire coursing through me. My arousal was evident as my pussy juices dripped and splattered onto the cold metal of the gun. I felt an intoxicating mix of power and vulnerability. With a firm grip, I lifted the revolver from the floor and cradled it in my hands, its weight adding to the intensity of the moment.

I don't know what it was, maybe it was the exhilaration coursing through my body, maybe it was the anticipation of reaching climax while he relentlessly devoured me with his skilled tongue, maybe it was the image of my own creamy release decorating the gun, but there was an electrifying surge that pumped through my veins. This encounter transcended mere sexual pleasure; it felt like I had stepped into a tantalizing film where I held the starring role. As I gazed at the gun resting in my palms once more, a mix of desire and danger coursed through me, intensifying the pulsating heat between us. I have handled a firearm on previous occasions and even pulled the trigger a few times, but let me be clear - I have never caused anyone's death. However, as I ran my fingers through his luscious Canadian hair - yes, he was indeed a Canadian - an unsettling curiosity arose within me. I found myself wondering what it would be like to end someone's life, to witness their final breath escaping their lips. I placed the gun against his skull, knowing that there was now a one in three chance of obliterating his head in a gruesome manner. A twisted smile crept across my face as I realized the depth of my depravity; this was some sick and twisted desire that consumed me entirely.

So now, it was time to step up my game. I had taken control of the situation, and I was determined to make the most of it. With a mischievous smile on my face, I whispered for him to go even deeper as he continued to pleasure me with his mouth. Suddenly, he looked at me with surprise and concern in his eyes.

"What the hell are you doing with that gun?" he exclaimed, his voice filled with a mix of fear and curiosity.

Without skipping a beat, I slowly brought the gun closer to his left temple, maintaining an air of dominance and control. Despite the dangerous nature of our actions, there was an undeniable thrill coursing through our veins. The adrenaline rush only heightened our senses and intensified the pleasure we derived from this twisted game we were playing. With a calm demeanour, I spun the cylinder of the gun, its metallic clicks providing an eerie soundtrack to our forbidden encounter. As fate would have it, the gun didn't fire. A wave of relief washed over us both as we locked eyes and shared a knowing smile.

Completely disregarding my presence, he persisted in draining every ounce of life from my body. Minutes later, he abruptly ceased his actions and rose to his feet. Walking back towards the window, he reached for his stash of cocaine and carefully lined up two perfect rails on a napkin. Returning to me, he spread my legs wide open and sprinkled the illicit substance directly onto my engorged clit. The gentle touch of the powder provided a strange sense of comfort to the sensitive area at the apex of my womanhood, as if numbing it from within. Without hesitation, he placed a lit cigarette between my lips and watched as I inhaled its toxic fumes.

I lay there in silence, the smoke from my cigarette curling lazily into the air. He knelt down before me once again, his eyes filled with desire. With a tender touch, he kissed the bottom of my feet, his lips lingering on each toe, igniting a pleasurable shiver throughout my body. As his mouth journeyed upwards, he dexterously traced patterns with his tongue along the length of my legs and thighs, teasing and tantalizing me with every stroke. Eventually, he arrived at the destination we both craved. Face to face with my vagina, he gazed at my vagina as if it were a precious work of art. His eyes locked onto her delicate folds, studying her contours and basking in her unique beauty. The white powder that adorned her surface was like an ethereal veil, making her even more alluring. Despite the obstacle it presented to him, he was undeterred by the challenge. With deliberate slowness and precision, he began to lick away the powder as if savouring a delectable treat. His tongue caressed my sensitive flesh with expertise and devotion, sending waves of pleasure coursing through me. I lay on the bed, completely captivated by his actions, lost in a world where only our desires mattered.

This was the deepest, scariest shit I have ever done in my life. The adrenaline coursed through my veins as I willingly embraced the danger. The thrill of the unknown mingled with the forbidden desires that consumed me. What if he did fire that gun? The thought sent a rush of excitement and fear cascading through my body. The possibility of my vagina being torn apart, fragmented into pieces, held an inexplicable allure. In that moment, I realized how much I craved the intensity and the pain. It was a twisted dance between pleasure and peril, where losing my pussy seemed like a small price to pay for such euphoria.

Now, I know the question you are about to ask, have I ever tried anything like this again? Fuck yes, who the hell do you think I am, some inexperienced novice? After that unforgettable day, it became my deepest desire, a craving that still consumes me to this day. The rush of pleasure, the intoxicating allure of surrendering control—it's an addiction that only grows stronger with each encounter. And let me tell you, he didn't just stop at my arm; he explored every inch of my body with a hunger that matched my own. My pussy may have been his primary focus, but he proved himself skilled in the art of oral pleasure as well. He devoured me with a fervour that left me trembling in ecstasy, so yes, this was now my fetish.

Sexual Masochism

Handcuff me to the bed and fucking torture me,
Legs up, eat my pussy then fuck me in a tree.
~

Scratch my back until I bleed,
Tie me up, make me plead.
Whisper in my ear, tell me what you'll do,
Slap my face and pull my hair too.
~

Take me to the edge and then let me fall,
I want it rough, I want it all.
Paddle my ass until it's red,
Bite my neck, leave marks instead.
~

Rip off my clothes and mark your territory,
Make me beg for more of your story.
Use your words like a weapon of seduction,
Make me forget all about caution.
~

Pullout your toys and show them to me,
Let's see which one will set us both free.
Kiss every inch of my skin with fire,
Push me harder, take me higher.
~

Don't stop until I'm begging for mercy,
The art of infliction, our favourite controversy.

Two

Bethany

I have carried these desires within me since I was a mere child, and yet they have always been shrouded in mystery and confusion. The complexity of my emotions perplexed me, leaving me unable to comprehend their origins. The incessant presence of these yearnings bewildered me; they consumed my thoughts relentlessly. Desperate for understanding, I sought ways to alleviate this inner turmoil, searching for an outlet to express myself. However, no matter how hard I tried to bury them deep within, they resurfaced with an intensity that defied all attempts to suppress them. In the depths of my mind, I frequently indulged in vivid fantasies of being dominated - someone's hands around my throat, their forceful grip pressing me against the wall as desperate cries for help escaped my lips.

I longed for a man who would push my boundaries, explore my darkest desires, and fulfil my need to be dominated. Someone who would understand that my cravings for pain and degradation were not a reflection of my self-worth, but rather an expression of my of handcuffs from the floor. Walking towards me, he commanded me to extend my arms as he securely fastened each cuff to the bed frame.

'Well damn,' I thought to myself, 'I think I am about to experience an intense rush of pleasure, no, like seriously mind-blowing this time. Thank you, universe, for the incredible sensations that await me.'

As my heart raced with anticipation, I couldn't help but marvel at the power of desire and exploration. As I lay there, bound and exposed on the bed, fear coursed through my veins. He returned to my side, his eyes filled with mischief and desire. Taking one final drag from his joint, he exhaled a cloud of smoke that mingled with the air around us. With a devilish grin, he removed the smouldering weed from his mouth, never breaking eye contact with me. And then, in a daring display of dominance, he placed the lit herb directly onto the sensitive flesh of my quivering vagina. The sensation was unlike anything I had ever experienced before - a delicious mix of heat and pleasure that sent shivers down my spine. The burning ember danced across my skin, leaving behind a trail of tingling sensations that ignited every nerve ending in my body. The mixture of pleasure and pain sent shockwaves throughout my body as I let out a primal scream, surrendering myself completely to his twisted desires.

"NO, STOP, PLEASE, NO FUCKING WAY," I yelled loudly, my voice filled with a mix of fear and anger. It had all become too much for me to handle - the pain, the degradation - I couldn't bear it any longer.

deepest sexual inclinations. And then, on that fateful day in January 2003, I met Ben. We were introduced by a mutual friend, and as we spent time together, I confided in him about my unconventional desires. To my relief, he didn't judge or recoil in horror; instead, he embraced me for who I truly was. With Ben, I found the freedom to explore the depths of my masochistic fantasies without fear or shame. He became not just a lover but also a trusted partner in the exploration of our shared passions.

Now, as he held me against the wall, his strong hand gripping my throat, I realized that this was not just a figment of my imagination. The intensity of his touch sent shivers down my spine and ignited an insatiable desire within me. My body responded eagerly, my clit throbbing with suspense, while my nipples hardened in response to the mix of fear and pleasure coursing through me. I longed to be taken to the edge, to experience the thrill of surrendering to his sadistic desires. I wondered if he would back away at the last moment, overwhelmed by the darkness that danced in his eyes. But there was something about his grip that made me believe he would follow through with his twisted fantasies. His hand tightened around my neck with a firmness that both excited and terrified me. In that moment, I knew I had found someone who understood my darkest desires.

As he continued to exert pressure on my throat, I couldn't help but wonder how far he would push me. Would he take me to places I had only fantasized about? The thought made my body ache with a mixture of trepidation and longing. I surrendered myself completely to him, eager to explore the depths of pleasure and pain that awaited us. In that moment, as his grip tightened even further, cutting off my breath momentarily, I knew that this encounter would be unlike any other. It was a journey into the realm of sexual masochism - a realm where pain and pleasure intertwine in a delicate dance. And in that momentary lack of oxygen, I felt alive like never before.

"Tighter," I whispered in his ears softly, and to my wish he responded.

His grip around me intensified, sending shivers down my spine. In that very moment, a wave of desire washed over me, as if surrendering to the pleasure that awaited. With a swift movement, he threw me onto the bed, his piercing gaze transforming into a mix of hunger and dominance. A slight pang of fear crept in, questioning my decision. But it was too late to turn back now; I had stepped into this realm willingly. Walking towards the bedside table, he retrieved a whip, its presence embodying a darker side of him that intrigued me even more.

"Turn the fuck around," he said in a very angry voice.

I couldn't help but feel a thrill of excitement as I complied with his command. The air crackled with a heady mix of desire and power, fuelling my excitement for the events that were about to unfold. However, my smile quickly faded when a piercing scream escaped my lips, the sound echoing through the room. In an instant, his hand struck my ass with a sharp sting, jolting me out of my reverie. Surprised by the suddenness of his action, I felt a rush of adrenaline course through my veins. Yet, despite the shock, fear was nowhere to be found within me. After all, this was exactly what I had been expecting - a journey into the depths of my own desires and pleasures. After a few minutes of getting lost in my thoughts, he started to whip me continuously. I closed my eyes tightly, surrendering to the sweet sting of pain that shot through my body with each strike. I then realized that the intensity of the sensations awakened something deep within me. It was a primal desire, a craving for the raw and unfiltered pleasure that could only be found in the realm of sexual masochism. As the whip landed on my skin, leaving behind red marks as evidence of our carnal connection, I couldn't help but wonder what it was about this particular form of pleasure that made me feel so alive. Was it the power exchange? The vulnerability? Or perhaps, it was simply the exquisite pleasure that came from pushing myself to new limits. Whatever it was, I knew one thing for certain - I wanted more.

"Oh, fuck yes harder, baby," I yelled, my voice filled with a mix of pleasure and desire.

The sound of my own words hung in the air, increasing the intensity of the moment. SMACK, this time he whipped me with such force that it sent a jolt through my body, causing me to gasp for breath. As the sting settled in, I could feel myself getting lost in the intoxicating pain. But even as I struggled to catch my breath, a part of me yearned for more. His actions were deliberate as he walked over to the bathroom, his steps echoing in the silence of the room. The sound of running water filled my ears as he turned on the faucet, preparing himself for what was to come next. The anticipation built within me as I lay there on my stomach, my ass exposed and waiting. Returning to me moments later, he stood tall and commanding above me. My eyes were drawn to his seven-inch cock dangling enticingly before me, a visual reminder of what was about to unfold. Without hesitation, he thrashed the whip across my back with a fervour that bordered on primal.

"You motherfucker," I yelled at the top of my lungs, the words reverberating through the room.

The anger and pain surged within me as I glared at him, my eyes filled with a mixture of defiance and vulnerability. I knew at that moment that my skin had bruised, but it was more than just physical marks that adorned my body. It was the deep wounds etched into my soul, the scars of submission and desire. As he stood there, a sadistic grin stretched across his face, he revelled in his power over me. The sound of his footsteps echoed in the silence as he hurried back to the bathroom. My heart raced with anticipation, knowing what awaited me next. This time, he didn't return empty-handed. In his hand was a belt buckle gleaming with malice and intent. The cold metal sent shivers down my spine as he approached, a wicked gleam in his eyes.

"Do you want some more?" he asked, tauntingly.

His voice dripped with cruel pleasure, fuelling a fire within me that I couldn't deny.

"Yes, motherfucker," I replied with defiant determination, embracing the darkness and surrendering to the intoxicating mix of pain and pleasure that consumed us both.

In that moment, boundaries blurred and inhibitions shattered as we delved deeper into our shared desires, lost in a world where passion knew no bounds. I knew very well that he was about to unleash a torrent of pain upon my flesh with the wet belt buckle, but I brushed off any concerns. This was something I had been yearning for since I could remember. In fact, I welcomed it with open arms, thinking to myself.

"Bring it on, you despicable person."

The belt buckle crashed down forcefully onto my exposed skin, repeatedly tormenting my backside. It ripped through the delicate layers, causing blood to flow freely from the deep wounds. No more tears could escape my eyes; they had all dried up. My body grew numb, rendering me speechless. Yet amidst the agony, I reminded myself that this was what I had craved. As the smacks continued relentlessly, each one landing with a sickening thud, I couldn't help but wonder how much more my body could endure. The pain was excruciating, yet strangely exhilarating at the same time. In that moment, it felt as though my very existence was defined by these agonizing blows. And then, suddenly, it happened. The final smack landed with such force that everything went dark. For a brief moment, I believed I had slipped into a coma, my consciousness fading away into oblivion. But as the haze cleared, I realized the truth - I was dead.

The brutality of his attack had taken its toll on my fragile mortal coil. Yet in his sadistic frenzy, he failed to notice that his victim was no longer conscious. It wasn't until he finally ceased his assault that I regained awareness of my surroundings. My senses slowly returned to me as I lay there motionless, listening to his heavy footsteps retreating towards the bedside table once again. And just when I thought the nightmare couldn't get any worse, he reached for his bag of cocaine and began sprinkling it onto the belt he had used to torment me.

Then, there was the final blow, as the drugs were meticulously sprinkled on the belt, causing a surge of fire to ripple through my body. The skin under my ass tingled with a mix of fear and desire, knowing what was about to come. As he tightened the belt around his hand, I braced myself for the intense sensations that awaited me. With precision and with one swift motion, he pulled the belt across my exposed flesh, igniting a searing pain that radiated through every nerve ending in my body. The intensity was overwhelming, yet strangely exhilarating. It was as if my senses had been heightened to a level I had never experienced before. And amidst the whirlwind of pleasure and pain, I found myself craving more, yearning for him to push me further into this abyss of ecstasy.

I watched in awe as he inhaled deeply, a mischievous grin spreading across his face before he sauntered back towards me. His hand clenched into a tight fist, growing larger and more menacing by the second. With a dominant presence, he positioned himself above me on the bed, his strong gaze penetrating my soul as he turned my body around. Meeting his intense, emerald eyes brought a fleeting sense of solace, but it was short-lived. The moment his gaze locked onto mine, all I felt was the relentless force of his fist repeatedly slamming into my ribs. The sheer weight and intensity of a one-hundred-and-eighty-pound man's punches were like an excruciatingly slow descent into death. No words could escape my mouth, no screams could pierce the air—only tears streamed down my face. It felt like a twisted dance of pleasure and pain, as if I were willingly submitting to my darkest desires. The tears that flowed from my eyes were not solely from the pain, but also from the intoxicating mixture of pleasure and vulnerability that consumed me.

I longed for him to stop, yet a part of me craved his dominance, his control over my body and soul. With each strike of his hand against my skin, the sensations rippled through me, igniting a fire within that I had never experienced before. It was an exquisite torment that awakened something primal deep within me. As he paused between strikes, his lips found mine in a tender kiss that held both tenderness and a hint of sadistic delight. And then, with the intensity of a storm subsiding, he shifted his focus to worshiping my body. His lips traced a path along every bruise he had inflicted upon me, turning pain into pleasure with each gentle touch. As he caressed my torso, his hands became instruments of healing, soothing the ache and leaving behind only traces of passion.

In those moments, I surrendered completely to him - body, mind, and soul. The lines between pain and pleasure blurred until they became one intoxicating sensation that consumed us both. It was in these moments of vulnerability and surrender that I discovered the true power of submission and the depths of pleasure that can be found in embracing our darkest desires. I felt a whirlwind of emotions coursing through me - confusion, humiliation, and drowsiness all tangled together. Never in my wildest dreams did I imagine that this man would take things to this extreme. I had yearned for this moment for so long, fantasizing about it since I was young, but now that it was happening, I couldn't help but question my own sanity. It was a twisted mix of pleasure and pain, desire and discomfort. And yet, despite feeling conflicted, I couldn't bring myself to utter the words to stop him. Deep down, a primal part of me craved more, knowing full well that there was no turning back now.

Taking no breaks, he stood up and walked off the bed, leaving me lying there, my ass burning from the relentless beating. He moved with purpose as he picked the belt back up and sprinkled more cocaine all over it, a twisted ritual that heightened his sadistic pleasure. Returning to me, he resumed the punishment with renewed vigor, each strike sending shockwaves of pain through my body. The cocaine acted as a cruel catalyst, intensifying both our sensations in this dark dance of pleasure and pain. As I lay there, my senses heightened by the sting of the drug on my flesh, I couldn't help but be drawn to his primal energy. He stood there, inhaling deeply, allowing the pungent aroma of cocaine to fill his lungs and intoxicate his senses. It was as if he was absorbing its power, letting it course through him like an elixir of darkness. After what felt like an eternity of torment, he finally relented.

Kneeling down before me, he leaned in close and sniffed every last trace of cocaine from my skin. His tongue followed suit, tracing lines across my body to ensure that none went to waste. It was a perverse act of devotion, a twisted communion between two souls lost in their shared desires. I watched him consume the remnants of the drug from my body with ravenous hunger, I realized how entangled we had become in this intricate web of pleasure and pain. The boundaries blurred as we surrendered ourselves to our darkest cravings, finding solace in each other's darkness.

I was completely taken aback, stunned by what was happening. It was as if he had done this countless times before, like he was an expert in the art of inflicting pleasure through pain. His actions were bold and daring, pushing boundaries I never thought I would explore. As he indulged in the forbidden pleasure of sniffing coke from my bootyhole, I couldn't help but surrender to his dominance. He knew exactly how to beat my ass into submission, silencing any doubts or resistance that lingered within me. This wasn't just substance abuse; it was a different kind of abuse altogether, one that awakened desires I didn't know existed. The pain became excruciating as he pushed me further, but my mind craved more even as my body cried out for mercy.

"Are you ready to submit to me?" he asked, his voice dripping with authority and desire.

I tried to slowly turn around, but the pain that shot through my body was overwhelming. It was as if every nerve ending was on fire, screaming for mercy. But in the depths of my being, I craved more. I yearned for the sweet release that only he could provide.

"I put it on my life" I replied.

I didn't even know why that came out of my mouth, but it was a testament to how much I desired him. It was as if my body and soul were screaming for you, craving every touch, every kiss, every intimate moment we shared. The intensity of our connection consumed me, igniting a fire within that I couldn't ignore. I knew deep down that this desire wasn't just about physical pleasure; it went beyond that. It was about exploring the depths of our desires together, pushing boundaries, and surrendering to the pleasures we both craved. With each touch, each strike, he took me to new heights of pleasure mingled with pain. My cries of ecstasy filled the room as I surrendered myself completely to his expert hands. I understood the true power of submission and the intoxicating allure of sexual exploration. He then forcefully flipped me over, and before I knew it, he was towering above me, his commanding presence sending shivers down my spine.

The sight of his impressive seven-inch member being thrust into my waiting mouth left me in awe. I struggled to keep up, the intensity overwhelming, as this encounter took on a whole new level of kinkiness. With each motion, he tantalizingly separated and reattached his cock from my eager lips, leaving me gasping for air. The beatings on my small white ass were nothing compared to the challenge of accommodating him deep within my throat. It was a test of endurance that pushed the boundaries of pleasure and pain, but one I couldn't resist taking on.

I tried desperately to utter the word "stop," but my voice failed me.

Frustration welled up inside me as I resorted to using my hands to pry his cock from my mouth. However, my feeble attempts were met with a firm grip, his left hand overpowering mine, rendering them useless. In that moment, I couldn't help but be amazed by his sheer strength. It was both intimidating and unsettling, adding another layer of fear to an already distressing situation. Tears streamed down my face as I began to cry uncontrollably, the overwhelming mix of emotions making it hard to breathe. As my body convulsed with coughs and the taste of bile filled my mouth, I realized I couldn't bear this any longer. The pain was too much for me to handle, both physically and emotionally. And finally, after what felt like an eternity, he seemed to grasp the gravity of the situation and ceased his actions. With a tender touch, he looked into my eyes and softly kissed me. His breathless words hung in the air as he asked if I wanted him to stop. In that moment, I felt a glimmer of hope that perhaps he understood the importance of consent and boundaries.

"No," I replied.

And there it was, I frightened myself with the realization of what I had gotten myself into. Why was I not stopping? What was wrong with me? Was I seeking some twisted form of validation? Not for him, but for my own desires and curiosity. As he picked up his joint from the ashtray and took a long drag, the room filled with a hazy tension. In the midst of the silence, he locked eyes with me, his gaze filled with an intoxicating mix of dominance and mischief. With a smirk on his lips, he reached down and retrieved two pairs

I pleaded with him to release me from the cuffs, desperate to put an end to this twisted game.

"WHAT THE FUCK MAN? Uncuff me right now!" I demanded, my voice trembling with a blend of defiance and desperation. "I'm not doing this with you anymore. Stop this shit right now!"

As his cold eyes stared back at me, a flicker of doubt seemed to pass over his face.

"Are you finished now?" he asked, perhaps sensing that something had changed within me.

And in that moment, a surge of strength flooded my veins. For the very first time in my life, I had finally reached my breaking point. I had endured enough pain and humiliation to last a lifetime. I realized that I didn't have to subject myself to this torment any longer. No more beatings, no more gagging. And certainly no more degrading acts that crossed every boundary of consent. Firmly asserting myself, I looked him straight in the eye and declared with unwavering determination.

"This ends now."

I slowly rose to my feet, every muscle in my body throbbing with pain. Gingerly, I made my way towards the bathroom, seeking solace and a moment of respite. As I gazed upon my reflection in the mirror, the sight of my bruised and battered skin was both unsettling and surreal. I turned around slowly, examining the aftermath of our encounter. Jagged wounds and raw abrasions adorned my body, serving as a painful reminder of the pleasure I had willingly subjected myself to. My eyes widened in disbelief as I noticed the remnants of our passionate encounter on my derriere, a stark contrast against my pale skin. The reality of what I had allowed myself to experience hit me like a tidal wave. A tumultuous mix of emotions washed over me as I questioned why I had chosen this path for myself.

"Because you wanted it, baby," he whispered seductively as he stealthily entered the dimly lit bathroom.

His sudden presence caught me off guard, and I could feel my heart racing. It was as if he had the ability to read my deepest desires without me even uttering a word. I couldn't help but wonder if he had somehow tapped into my thoughts. Without wasting a moment, he pulled me into his arms, pressing his body against mine. Our eyes met in the mirror, intensifying the electric connection between us. In that instant, a surge of longing coursed through my veins, and I yearned for him in ways I never thought possible. The desire to surrender myself to his dominance consumed me entirely.

"Are you ready for more, baby?" he asked, his voice laced with a mixture desire.

I met his gaze, feeling a surge of arousal course through me. The words that had been trapped within me finally found their release in a soft moan. His hand found mine, fingers intertwining as he led me back into the bedroom. With each step, the excitement grew, knowing that I was about to experience something beyond my wildest fantasies. As he guided me onto the bed, my heart raced with a mix of nervousness and exhilaration. My limbs were gently bound, the sensation of being restrained heightening my senses. I reveled in the feeling of vulnerability and surrender, knowing that this was where I truly belonged. This wasn't just a fleeting moment;

it was an awakening to a part of myself that craved submission and pleasure.

With every touch and caress, he awakened desires I never knew existed. His lips explored every inch of my body, leaving me breathless and hungry for more. As his mouth found its way to my most intimate places, I surrendered completely to the ecstasy that awaited me. In that moment, as pleasure surged through my veins, I realized that this wasn't just about physical gratification—it was about embracing the depths of my desires. And as I gave in to the intoxicating rhythm between us, I knew that this addiction would forever be etched into my soul.

The Alaskan Pipeline

The Alaskan pipeline, they call it so,
A thrill that comes with a whiskey flow.

~

Pushed to the edge, I feel it in my veins,
My body aches for the pleasure and pains.

~

I'll relax in a setting, sipping on wine,
As we explore each other's bodies divine.

~

With every thrust, we reach new heights,
Our passion ignites, burning bright.

~

Sweat glistening on our skin so bare,
Moans and gasps fill the air.

~

We move together in perfect rhythm,
Exploring each other's fantasies and whims.

~

Shit gets real nasty, but we can't deny,
The pleasure that comes when we both try.

~

Through pleasure and pain, we'll make it through,
This is our love, raw and true.

Three

Alicia

"Baby," I murmured softly, my gaze fixed on his penetrating eyes, "I long for your presence. The nights without you have become unbearable."

With a hint of regret in his voice, he replied, "I understand, my love. But you know the circumstances. I must go."

Frustration welled up within me as I pleaded, "How much longer must we endure this separation? How many more nights will we be apart?"

Helplessly, he asked, "What can I do?"

In an attempt to lighten the mood, I teased.

"Well, you can leave behind all the unnecessary baggage and just bring your manhood with you."

See, the naked man sitting before me was not mine. In fact, he was a married man with kids. I found myself caught up in his secret affair, playing the role of his little side baby. And truth be told, I revelled in that clandestine excitement. However, the situation had become exhausting. Our encounters were fleeting, and each time he satisfied me, he had to rush back to his wife and business. I grew weary of this cycle and craved a change with every fiber of my being. Frustrated, I voiced my discontent.

"Well, perhaps I should just find someone else to satisfy my needs,"

I moaned in exasperation. But before my words could fully escape my lips, he gently slapped my left cheek as if to silence me. The gesture spoke volumes: I was to shut up and refrain from speaking such nonsense.

"Don't you ever say that," he warned with a seriousness that sent shivers down my spine. "You knew what the deal was from the beginning."

It was a surreal situation I found myself in, tangled up in a web of desire and longing. We had been caught in a whirlwind romance, fuelled by passion and forbidden love. But now, reality had set in and we had to face the consequences of our actions. He looked at me with desperation in his eyes, his voice filled with anguish as he questioned what else could be done. I realized the depth of his love for me, despite the circumstances. And as much as it pained me to admit it, I knew that a mere sex toy wouldn't solve our problems.

"Use a fucking dildo, Alicia, what else can you do? You want me to cut off my penis and give it to you is that it?" he yelled.

"I mean it would help," I replied.

"You know what, I have an idea," he said.

"Have you ever heard about the Alaskan pipeline?" he asked as he put on his t-shirt.

"No, what the fuck is that?" I responded.

Intrigued, I listened as he slowly explained the concept to me. It was a method of sexual gratification that involved using a frozen dildo made from his shit.

"No way am I going to try that, Dave. Are you out of your mind? I am not using your shit as a dick, are you fucking insane?" I exclaimed, flinging something at him in disbelief.

Dave chuckled and replied, "Nah, I'm perfectly fine. It's just you always nagging me about trying new things. Come on, what else do you want me to do?"

As he leaned in to kiss me, my initial anger subsided a bit. His lips pressed against mine, and he began kissing me slowly, tracing a path from my stomach. As his lips left my stomach, he slowly moved down to my neck, tracing delicate patterns with his tongue. The warmth of his touch made me shiver, igniting a fire within me. I couldn't help but surrender to the passion that consumed us both. With each kiss, he explored every inch of my body, leaving me breathless and craving for more. His skilled tongue danced across my skin, teasing and tantalizing me with every movement. I arched my back in ecstasy as he expertly found his way back down to my stomach, leaving a trail of desire in his wake. The intensity of our connection grew with every passing second, as we lost ourselves in a world of pleasure and desire. Our bodies moved together in perfect harmony, creating a symphony of moans and whispers that echoed throughout the room.

Caught up in the moment, I realized that Dave had a knack for pushing boundaries and introducing me to new experiences. Despite my initial resistance, there was an undeniable thrill in exploring uncharted territory with him. But as our passionate encounter continued, I couldn't help but wonder about the practicality of the Alaskan pipeline he had mentioned earlier. Was freezing bodily waste really a thing? And more importantly, did anyone actually do it? These questions lingered in the back of my mind as we lost ourselves in the heat of the moment. Afterward, as we lay tangled together under the sheets, I found myself contemplating the balance between adventure and sanity. While Dave's ideas could sometimes be outrageous and unconventional, they also forced me to question societal norms and embrace my own desires.

I woke up that morning frustrated, not knowing when the hell I would see him again. The anticipation was driving me crazy, and I couldn't help but crave his presence. My desire for him consumed my thoughts, overshadowing any rationality or self-control. As I got ready for the day, I couldn't shake off the memory of what he had done. It disgusted me, yet the pull towards him was too strong to resist. Taking a long shower, I tried to wash away both my physical and emotional attachment to him. But no matter how hard I scrubbed, his image lingered in my mind. And then there was his wife - that big fat dinosaur of a woman who he had chosen over me. She was far from attractive, resembling an American Pitbull with her size and sour expression. The thought of her being with him made me sick with jealousy and resentment. Despite all the pain and frustration of being the "other woman," I couldn't deny the intense love I felt for him. It was a complicated situation that left me feeling torn between desire and self-respect.

As I walked downstairs in my towel, I opened the freezer door, staring at it for a few seconds. I couldn't believe what I was about to do. With a mix of curiosity and excitement, I carefully removed the frozen package from the freezer and made my way back upstairs into my bedroom. The anticipation was palpable as I laid on the bed, ensuring that every inch of me was wonderfully comfortable. Taking a deep breath, I unwrapped the package and placed it gently on the bed. This was uncharted territory for me, an experience unlike anything I had ever tried before. Little did I know that this unconventional act, known as an Alaskan pipeline, would awaken sensations within me that surpassed even those of his actual dick.

As I sat on the bed, my gaze fixated on his impressive creation wrapped in the condom. It was a magnificent specimen, firm and unyielding, begging to be explored further. With a sense of hope, I spread my legs open wide, creating space for the rock-hard faeces to find its rightful place inside me. Slowly and deliberately, I inserted it, relishing in the sensations that coursed through my body. Closing my eyes, I allowed myself to surrender to the fantasy unfolding in my mind. In that moment, it wasn't just faecal matter filling me; it was him - the embodiment of desire and pleasure. The intensity grew as I indulged in self-pleasure, thrusting with fervour and abandon. Each movement heightened the connection between us, blurring the lines between reality and imagination.

The experience took an unexpected turn as I decided to taste this embodiment of our passion. Removing it from my vagina, I brought it to my lips without hesitation. With every lick and suck, I revelled in the forbidden act, intertwining pleasure and taboo. My breasts became an extension of this erotic dance as I teased and caressed them with one hand. I relished every moment, savouring both the physical and psychological gratification that came with embracing this unconventional desire. There was no judgment or shame; only pure unadulterated pleasure cascading through my being.

With every rough thrust, my body violently accepted his waste inside of me, the flimsy barrier of the condom bursting under the pressure. A mixture of revulsion and ecstasy flooded through my veins as I used my dildo to force it even deeper into my core. The sensation of it melting and mingling with my own fluids sent waves of intense pleasure coursing through every inch of my being. Laying on the bed, consumed by my insatiable desires, I couldn't help but revel in the taboo act that brought me such intense satisfaction. As I sat on the toilet later, feeling his excrement slide out of me with ease, a strange sense of longing took over. No longer did I miss him when we met up - he always left gifts now, but nothing compared to the thrill of his new gift to me: his scat-covered condom. The taste and scent of him lingered on my tongue and in my mind long after he was gone, driving me wild with desire. I would rush home just to freeze this twisted reminder of our depraved encounters, never wanting to let go of this new fetish that brought such intense pleasure and satisfaction to my dark desires.

Edge Play

It wasn't merely a fanciful notion,
I inhabited it, I experienced it, I could sense the emotion.
~

My physique was strong, but my member yearned for action,
Now stroke that organ, as I release my satisfaction.
~

Desire flows, crimson dripping as you pleasure my core,
When that needle punctures me, visions start to pour.
~

No anger or annoyance, reveal that phallus and apply the lotion,
Now let's unite and transform this kink into devotion.

Four

Michael

I came home from university that day, stressed out and not in the fucking mood. The weight of exams and assignments was suffocating me, leaving little room for patience or socializing. All I wanted was some peace and quiet to decompress. As I entered the house, I could feel the tension melt away momentarily, only to be replaced by a growling hunger. My low blood sugar levels intensified my already erratic emotions, making me even more irritable.

In an attempt to alleviate my hunger pangs, I dropped my bag on the floor and rushed up the stairs. However, what greeted me was not the solitude I craved but a symphony of loud music and unmistakable moaning sounds echoing through the walls. My initial thought was that it must be my father indulging in some late-night pleasure, but quickly dismissed it as he was still at work. His long hours were typical for someone running his own finance company. He always came home late, and my mother worked for a broker company, and she was on a business trip, leaving me alone in the house. As I sat in my room, trying to distract myself from the eerie silence, I suddenly heard strange noises coming from upstairs. My heart raced in my chest as I cautiously made my way up the stairs, unsure of what awaited me.

Fear consumed me as the noises grew louder and more distinct, emanating from my parents' room. My mind raced with possibilities - was it an intruder? A deranged stranger? I quickly retreated downstairs, my hands trembling as I reached for a knife from the kitchen. Although I knew it wasn't the wisest decision to confront whoever was upstairs, fear had overridden rational thought. With every step towards their room, I braced myself for the unknown, determined to uncover the truth behind those unsettling sounds. As I cautiously made my way out of the kitchen, gripping the nine-inch knife tightly in my trembling hands, my eyes fell upon the vacant wine stand. It struck me with disbelief that a few bottles were now missing from its usual display. The audacity of these intruders astounded me. Did they truly have the nerve to pilfer my parents' prized wine collection? A surge of adrenaline coursed through my veins, causing my heart to pound so fiercely I could almost hear it echo in my ears. Sweat formed on my palms, making it increasingly difficult to maintain a firm grasp on the weapon.

My mind raced with a whirlwind of thoughts, each one more chaotic than the last. Who were these people? Why would they target our home? Were they merely seeking a place for illicit rendezvous or was there more to their intentions? It was inconceivable that someone would risk breaking into our house for a mere three bottles of wine. My parents' bed flashed before my eyes, a reminder of past indiscretions that had taken place within its comforting embrace. The realization began to sink in that this intrusion held deeper implications than initially perceived. There was an unsettling sense of violation and vulnerability that enveloped the air around me. As I stood there, knife clenched tightly, I vowed to unearth the truth and bring justice to those who dared disturb the sanctity of our home.

Let me tell you this right now, I was born a freak, I have eaten ass, sucked toes, licked earlobes, but let me assure you that what I witnessed that day was beyond anything I could have imagined. As I stood outside my parents' bedroom door, my eyes widened with each passing second. The sight before me was surreal. My father, usually a pillar of strength and authority, was rendered helpless and vulnerable. He was restrained to the bed, his limbs bound tightly. A gag covered his mouth, muffling any sound he might attempt to make. His body lay exposed and defenceless, an unsettling contrast to his usual commanding presence. The tip of his erect member peeked through the restraints, a symbol of both desire and humiliation. I was in complete shock as I stood there, unable to believe what my eyes were witnessing. My father, whom I had always known as a strong and dignified man, was now restrained to his bed with handcuffs on his arms and legs.

The sight of him, vulnerable and exposed, sent a wave of confusion and disbelief coursing through my veins. As if that wasn't enough, his mouth was tightly strapped shut with some kind of sexual apparatus, leaving him completely silenced. It was a disturbing scene, one that I never thought I would witness in my own home. And then there was the woman in the room, who bore an uncanny resemblance to my mother. However, her face was concealed behind a doctor's mask, preventing me from seeing her true identity or intentions. The whole situation seemed surreal and left me grappling for answers. Who was this mysterious woman? What could have led to such a horrifying scenario? These questions raced through my mind as I tried to make sense of the chaos unfolding before me.

The woman exuded confidence as she strutted in her pink knee-high boots, paired with alluring lingerie that accentuated her curves. It was undeniable that her double-D breasts were showcased through her brassiere, leaving little to the imagination. In disbelief, I couldn't fathom that this seductive figure could possibly be my mother. Our attempts to discuss matters of intimacy had always been met with discomfort and avoidance on her part, leading me to seek guidance from my father instead. Yet here she was, engaged in a passionate encounter with him. As I stood there, a silent observer to this unexpected scene, my eyes widened when the lady approached the bedside table and picked up what appeared to be a needle. Intrigue gripped me as I pondered what her next move might be.

Now what the fuck was she about to do with that? I wondered. As I watched her, my curiosity grew. She approached my father with a determined stride, climbing onto the bed and positioning herself directly over his face. With a swift motion, she removed the leather mouth strap that had restricted his speech. And then, something unexpected happened - she sat on his face. My father eagerly welcomed her, his mouth wide open, ready to pleasure her in any way she desired. It was a shocking sight to witness, seeing my strict and uncompromising father willingly submit to my mother's desires while restrained. As she grinded and whined on top of him, I couldn't help but feel a mix of confusion and fascination. How had things come to this point in their relationship? Had they always harboured such hidden desires? The image before me shattered the perception I had of them as conventional parents. They were exploring a realm of intimacy that I could never have imagined.

Meanwhile, there she was, still holding the needle in her hand. It struck me that this act of dominance and submission was just one facet of their complex dynamic. Perhaps it was an expression of trust and vulnerability between them - a unique way for them to connect on a deeper level. In that moment, I realized that human sexuality is far more intricate than we often perceive it to be. It isn't always confined within societal norms or expectations. People are capable of embracing their deepest desires and finding fulfilment in unconventional ways. As I continued to observe this intimate scene unfolding before me, I couldn't help but question my own under-standing of love and relationships. How well did I truly know the people closest to me? And how willing was I to explore the depths of my own desires?

This unexpected encounter between my parents served as a re-minder that life is filled with surprises and complexities beyond our imagination. It taught me not to judge others based on appearances or societal expectations, but rather to embrace the diverse expres-sions of love and intimacy that exist in the world. As I observed from a distance, a mischievous grin formed on my face. It was quite an intimate scene unfolding before my eyes. Without missing a beat, she smoothly glided her hand down his body, reaching the lower regions. In her other hand, she held a bottle of sensuous oil, ready to enhance their experience. With a flick of her wrist, she let the oil cascade over his skin, creating a slippery sensation. The bottle dropped to the floor as she skilfully used her hands to spread the oil all over him. The anticipation in my father's eyes was evi-dent as he braced himself for what was to come next. Approaching his manhood with confidence, she applied just the right amount of pressure while keeping up a rhythmic motion. Holding onto him firmly, she gazed at his member with a mix of desire and control unravelled in her eyes.

She then gently caressed his thighs with her left hand, lavishing attention on his penis, providing it with a sense of comfort and security. She demonstrated her unwavering devotion to his manhood, assuring it of her eternal love. Taking her time, she adeptly maneuverer her hands around his member, exerting a gentle pressure that allowed the blood to circulate freely through his lower extremities. With delicate precision and without any contact to her teeth, she released a small amount of saliva from her mouth, creating a sensual sensation as it cascaded over his throbbing cock. Observing intently, I couldn't help but notice that my father was uncircumcised, and this alluring woman took special care to cater to his unique anatomy.

She continued to handle his member with a delicate yet firm touch, aware of the sensitivity of his uncircumcised state. Taking care not to cause any discomfort, she expertly worked her way around his shaft, providing him with an intense and pleasurable experience. As the minutes passed, I couldn't help but notice the sheer passion and intensity in my father's moans as he reached the peak of pleasure. It was clear that my mother possessed a deep understanding of his desires and knew exactly how to satisfy them. Her body moved with grace and confidence, exuding a seductive energy that was impossible to ignore. This woman, whom I affectionately refer to as my mother, was an undeniable expert in the art of lovemaking. She had years of experience under her belt, which she effortlessly demonstrated through her every move.

"Are you ready, baby?" she purred seductively, her voice dripping with desire.

He gazed into her eyes, his own filled with anticipation.

"More than I will ever be," he whispered, his voice filled with longing.

In a bold move, she grasped his throbbing manhood with one hand. With the other hand, she skillfully administered the injection into his erect member. A mixture of pleasure and pain surged through his body as he let out an involuntary cry. The room seemed to spin around him as he struggled to comprehend what was happening. The initial excitement quickly morphed into a sense of danger as he realized the situation had taken a dark turn. Panic gripped him as he tried to make sense of the unfolding events. Driven by a primal urge, he begged for more, surrendering himself completely to her control. His pleas were met with another needle produced from her hidden stash, this time aimed at the sensitive base of his engorged penis.

As the needle pierced his skin, a wave of ecstasy mingled with agony washed over him. Every nerve in his body electrified with both pleasure and trepidation. The room fell silent except for their heavy breathing and the faint sound of blood pumping through their veins. The intensity of their shared experience hung in the air like an invisible bond between them. In that moment, they existed within a realm where boundaries blurred and inhibitions faded away. They had embarked on a journey that would forever change them, bound together by a potent mixture of desire and danger.

"Mother fucker, you amazing dumb bitch, ARGGG, oh my god," he continued to yell, as blood began to develop from his penis.

She then stood up and walked towards him, a wicked smile playing on her lips. With a swift movement, she retrieved another needle from her bra and approached his right ear. The anticipation in the room was palpable as she pierced his ear with the needle. His screams filled the air as he writhed in agony. Yet, amidst the chaos, she leaned closer to him and whispered those three words that held such power.

"I love you."

The intensity of his screams only grew louder as he responded with equal fervor:

"I love you too!"

Tears streamed down his face as he pleaded for mercy. It was a desperate plea that fell on deaf ears, for she was consumed by her own twisted desires. In the midst of this horrifying scene, I couldn't help but mutter under my breath.

"Yeah, no more... This crazy bitch is killing my father." My voice barely audible amidst the chaos.

The room reeked of pain and desperation as her actions continued to inflict torment upon him. The sheer audacity of her actions left me stunned. As blood pooled around him and his cries echoed through the room, it became clear that this was a nightmare he would never wake up from. What the hell was going on with my parents? Could this be some sort of mid-life crisis they were both experiencing? It baffled me to think about what could possibly go through someone's mind to make them act so absurdly.

It was truly outrageous. As I observed their antics in utter disgust, I couldn't help but admit that there was a tiny part of me that found it strangely amusing. Despite my low pain tolerance, if my father could engage in such bizarre behavior without having a heart attack, then surely I could endure this nonsense as well, right? I wondered if they had lost touch with reality or if there was something deeper at play here. These thoughts swirled around in my head, leaving me feeling both perplexed and intrigued.

With blood pouring from his body, she carefully lifted the lit candle in her right hand, illuminating the room with a soft glow. In a moment of quiet intensity, she positioned herself above him once more, slowly lowering herself onto his face, inviting him to savor her like a delectable fruit cake. Despite the pain that coursed through him, my father remained steadfast and unwavering throughout this extraordinary encounter. Moments later, she turned around, her back facing him, and without hesitation, instructed him to explore the depths of her anus with his eager mouth. Her left hand gracefully reached behind her and spread open her buttocks, exposing the intimate recesses for his pleasure. As she closed her eyes and surrendered to the exquisite sensations of his tongue caressing her innermost desires, a satisfied smile danced across her lips while she gently nibbled on her bottom lip.

As she delicately held the candle in her hand, a mischievous smile played on her lips. She couldn't resist the temptation to explore new sensations with her lover. Slowly, she began dripping the warm wax all over his torso, watching as it traced intricate patterns on his skin. His moans of pleasure echoed through the room, powering her desire to push boundaries even further.

"Hmmm, oh shit," he moaned, unable to contain his excitement.

"Don't stop eating that ass," she replied seductively, her voice laced with a hint of mischief.

The combination of their forbidden act and the sensual play with wax heightened their pleasure to unimaginable heights.

"I won't baby," he murmured passionately, his words punctuated by short breaks as he tried to communicate while indulging in the feast before him. "I love this ass so much, I'm going to savour it for the rest of my life."

As the wax continued to drip onto his skin, I watched in disbelief as my mother once again reached for his penis. My mind immediately went to the possibility of her performing oral sex on him, reminiscent of a sixty-nine position that I quite enjoy myself. However, much to my surprise, she didn't do that. Instead, she held the flame dangerously close to his member. Within seconds, the piercing sound of my father's agonized screams filled the room.

"MOTHERFUCKER, WHAT THE FUCK!" His words reverberated through the air, causing me to jump in sheer astonishment.

The suddenness of it all was enough to make me lose control and release a small amount of urine into my pants. The scene before me was like something out of a nightmare. The pain etched on my father's face was palpable, his body writhing in agony as the wax burned his sensitive skin. I couldn't tear my eyes away from the horrifying spectacle unfolding before me. My mother's actions were beyond comprehension. How could she do this to him? What kind of sick pleasure did she derive from inflicting such pain? It was as if I was witnessing a twisted form of torture right in front of my eyes.

The atmosphere in the room was thick with tension and fear. The once peaceful and loving environment had been shattered by this shocking act of cruelty. I felt a mixture of anger and helplessness welling up inside me, unsure of what I could do to stop this madness. In that moment, I realized that things would never be the same again. The trust and love that once existed between my parents had been irreparably damaged. And as I stood there, trembling with both fear and disgust, I couldn't help but wonder how we had reached this point - a point where our family had become engulfed in darkness and despair. No longer able to bear witness to the horrifying scene unfolding before me, I turned away, my heart pounding with fear and confusion.

How could someone inflict such pain and suffering? The stench of burning flesh filled the air, a nauseating reminder of the agony being inflicted upon my father. I felt a deep sense of unease, not only for him but for myself as well. It was as if I had stumbled upon a dark secret, an evil lurking within the walls of our home. Despite the overwhelming urge to flee, I found myself rooted in place, compelled to continue watching. Perhaps it was morbid curiosity or a desperate need for answers, but I couldn't tear my eyes away from the grotesque spectacle playing out before me.

She then switched positions, picked my father's penis back up and placed it inside of her anus.

"Oh wow, yes baby, let me fuck that fat ass," groaned my father.

As I observed the scene unfolding before me, it became apparent that this woman, whom I hesitantly call my mother, did not possess a curvaceous posterior.

'I suppose carnal desires can prompt men to utter absurdities,' I contemplated silently.

In the midst of their passionate encounter, my father's exclamations seemed disconnected from reality. It was as though his primal urges had momentarily overridden his senses. The intensity of the moment was undeniable, and it made me question the boundaries of human desire. The rawness and fervor in their actions hinted at a profound connection between them, transcending physical appearances. As an outsider peering into their intimate world, I couldn't help but ponder the intricacies of love and lust that often elude our comprehension. She continued to passionately engage in intimate relations with my father, her movements becoming even more enticing. The sight of their intense connection only heightened my own arousal, causing my already erect member to become rock solid.

Overwhelmed by desire, I instinctively reached down and discreetly slipped my hand into my pants, relishing the sensation of stroking myself slowly. The need for release grew stronger with each passing moment, urging me to retreat to the privacy of my room for some much-needed self-pleasure. Reluctantly tearing my gaze away from the captivating scene unfolding before me, I left my parents to attend to their own desires while I attended to mine. As I made my way towards my sanctuary, a sudden sound reverberated through the house - the front door creaking open. My curiosity piqued, I cautiously peered down the stairs, wondering who could be arriving at this late hour.

"ANDY," my mother's voice echoed through the house as she entered, her shopping bags thudding onto the floor.

My father remained oblivious to her presence. I glanced at my mother, then back at the woman who shamelessly allowed my father to indulge in eating her ass. I glanced at my mother, then shifted my gaze towards the unfamiliar woman who was shamelessly allowing my father to indulge in her backside.

"Wow, this woman certainly has an appetite for a peculiar kind of pleasure," I mused silently.

In that bewildering moment, I paused to grasp the reality of the situation. Who was this woman? How did she manage to infiltrate our lives and corrupt my father's fidelity? It dawned on me, with a mix of horror and disbelief, that this devilish creature was not my own mother. As the pieces fell into place, I couldn't help but exclaim in utter shock.

"Holy shit! That's not my goddamn mother!" The realization left me questioning everything.

How could my father betray our family with such audacity? And who was this sinister seductress who had ensnared him? With a surge of anger and confusion coursing through me, I vowed to unravel the truth behind this scandalous affair. It was time to confront both my father and this mysterious woman who dared to invade our home and tear our family apart.

"ANDY!" my mother's voice echoed through the house once again.

Startled, my father's body jolted upright in complete astonishment. It was as if he had heard a divine call, a command that demanded his immediate attention. As I observed their interaction, a thought crossed my mind - perhaps my father felt a surge of adrenaline, as if he were being summoned by a higher power. But deep down, I couldn't help but question how he would meet his demise today. Would it be a fatal stabbing? Or perhaps he would be strangled to death? The uncertainty weighed heavily on my mind. What I did know for certain is that if my mother were to discover him in bed with this woman, he would be doomed.

My dad quickly struggled to get off the bed, but he couldn't, his hands were still tightly cuffed to the bed. I watched as the lady, clad in knee-high boots, frantically searched for the key to free my father from the handcuffs. With a sense of urgency, she finally managed to unlock them and my dad let out a sigh of relief. As she started to remove her mask, I couldn't help but feel a mix of anticipation and anxiety. Who was behind this elaborate scheme? As her face was revealed, my heart sank. It was someone I never expected - my own fiancé. The realization hit me like a ton of bricks. How could she betray me like this? How long had she been deceiving me? Questions swirled in my mind as I stood there in disbelief, struggling to comprehend the magnitude of her betrayal. For an entire hour, I remained outside my father's room, silently observing the woman I thought I knew so well, now exposed as a stranger with ulterior motives.

I stood frozen outside my father's room, my heart pounding in my chest. The image of my girlfriend, the woman I thought I knew so well, pleasuring my own father was seared into my mind. It was as if the world had turned upside down in an instant, shattering all the trust and love we had built over the years. I couldn't tear my eyes away from the shocking scene unfolding before me, a twisted nightmare I never could have imagined. As she knelt before him, her lips wrapped around his throbbing member, I felt a mix of anger, disgust, and betrayal wash over me. How could she stoop so low? How could he betray our family in such a despicable manner? The sight of her swallowing every last drop of his essence made bile rise in my throat.

My mother's footsteps echoed up the stairs, breaking the surreal spell that had held me captive. Panic surged through me, urging me to hide or flee from this abomination. But something compelled me to stay rooted to the spot. Maybe it was morbid curiosity or a desperate need for answers. Time seemed to stretch as I grappled with what I should do next. Should I confront them? Should I expose their sordid affair? Or should I retreat and pretend none of this ever happened?

The weight of these decisions bore down on me like a suffocating burden. In that moment, standing outside that room filled with betrayal and twisted desires, everything changed. The innocence and naivety that once coloured our relationship were shattered beyond repair. My world had been irrevocably altered by this unimaginable act of infidelity. And as my mind raced with conflicting emotions. In that moment, I knew I should have turned away and pretended not to see what was happening. But something held me there, unable to move or even breathe. My mother came running up the stairs as my father continued to free himself, but it was too late, they messed up this time.

"Michael, Michael, are you okay?" my mother exclaimed, concern evident in her voice.

I remained silent, unable to find the words to respond, my eyes fixated on both my father and the despicable ex-fiancé standing before me. My mother stood there, her face a mixture of confusion and disbelief.

"Debra," my dad uttered in complete shock, his voice trembling with a combination of anger and sadness.

"Michael, I'm so sorry," my ex-fiancé pleaded, her voice filled with regret and desperation.

She tried to explain herself, but I couldn't bring myself to listen. The betrayal was too fresh, the pain too deep. I stood there in silence, not because I wanted an explanation, not because I felt betrayed by both my father and soon to be wife, but because I couldn't comprehend the depths of their deceit. It was as if my world had shattered into a million pieces, each fragment cutting deeper into my soul. The images replayed in my mind like a haunting film, tormenting me with every frame. I could still hear their laughter echoing in the room, mocking the trust I had placed in them. A wave of nausea washed over me, threatening to consume me whole.

With every step towards the bathroom, my heart pounded louder, matching the rhythm of my racing thoughts. Tears streamed down my face uncontrollably, mingling with the taste of bitterness that lingered on my tongue. In that moment, I realized that this betrayal was not just about infidelity; it was a betrayal of everything I held dear - love, loyalty, and the belief that family meant something. As I splashed cold water on my face, trying to wash away the pain, a newfound determination ignited within me. No longer would I allow myself to be defined by their actions; it was time for me to reclaim my own happiness and rebuild the shattered pieces of my life.

It has been an eternity since I last laid eyes on or received any form of communication from my father. Please refrain from inquiring about that despicable woman. As for her whereabouts and activities, I am as ignorant as can be. Frankly, I cannot say with certainty whether she is alive or deceased; in my mind, she has long been dead, rendering her existence inconsequential. However, if you are curious as to why I find myself bound and restrained upon this bed, that is an entirely different tale altogether.

Cunnilingus Master

I flicked it, I kissed it, and oh, how that pussy did start,
In the cozy confines of a hotel room, we played our part.
The atmosphere was clean, with decor that never had a smell,
As I sucked on her clit so hard, an erotic tale began to tell.

~

Her delicate bud responded eagerly to my skilled touch,
A symphony of pleasure in that intimate space we did clutch.
With each flick of my tongue, she writhed in sweet ecstasy,
Moans escaping her lips as she surrendered completely.

~

Not content with just her clit, I explored further below,
I ventured to that forbidden place where few dare to go.
And yes, I licked that bootyhole too, breaking all taboos,
Because in the heat of passion, there's nothing we won't choose.

~

In the depths of desire, boundaries cease to exist,
We indulged in pleasures untamed and could not resist.
So there we were, in that hotel room's passionate embrace,
Lost in each other's bodies, creating a memory time cannot
erase.

Five

Mike

I was twenty-five and single, mobile apps weren't a thing, but I had found myself on a website that connected people for casual encounters. To my surprise, I actually got a match and we started exchanging messages. She turned out to be a genuine person, a twenty-two-year-old university student pursuing her Master's degree in a city not too far from me. It was clear that she was looking for some excitement as she suggested meeting at a hotel halfway between our locations. After a brief conversation and some gentle persuasion, I agreed to drive to the hotel despite the late hour. The eagerness in me grew as I hit the road, wondering what this encounter would bring.

The thought of meeting someone new in such an unconventional way excited me and filled me with curiosity. As I drove closer to the hotel, my heart raced with both nervousness and anticipation. Little did I know what awaited me on the other side of that hotel room door...

The night porter at the hotel already knew that a guest was expected, so gaining access to the famous hotel chain was a breeze. As I walked down the corridor to the room, a mix of excitement and apprehension filled my mind. Was she a catfish? Her picture portrayed her as stunning, but it was just a face shot. I couldn't help but wonder if she would live up to my expectations or if there was more than met the eye. Was she hiding something? My fingers nervously tapped on the door, and to my surprise, it swung open almost immediately. And there she stood, a vision of beauty. A slender figure, draped in nothing but a pair of seductive black panties. My heart skipped a beat as I took in her exquisite features and alluring confidence. It was impossible not to be captivated by her presence. And yet, amidst the overwhelming desire that coursed through my veins, a lingering doubt remained.

Could this be too good to be true? Was there something hidden beneath her flawless facade? But in that moment, none of it mattered. As our eyes locked and an electric energy filled the air between us, doubts and uncertainties faded away. The allure of her beauty consumed me entirely, leaving me yearning for what lay ahead. It was clear that this encounter would be anything but ordinary. In that instant, I knew one thing for certain - this night would forever be etched in my memory as an unforgettable chapter in my life's novel of passion and desire.

As the door closed behind me, enveloping us in a world of intimacy, our bodies instinctively gravitated towards one another. Our lips collided in a passionate embrace, igniting a fire within us that threatened to consume everything else. The taste of her mouth was like sweet nectar, driving my desire to explore every inch of her being. With each kiss, our tongues engaged in a sensual dance, teasing and tantalizing one another. My hands, guided by an insatiable curiosity, ventured down her back, tracing the contours of her spine before finding their resting place on her pert ass cheeks. The softness of her skin beneath my fingertips sent shivers down my spine. A mischievous smile played upon her lips as she beckoned me towards the bed. With grace and confidence, she positioned herself against the headboard, her legs spread wide apart, inviting me to indulge in the depths of her desire. I knew that this encounter was about more than just physical pleasure; it was an exploration of passion and connection.

Time seemed to stand still as I gazed into her eyes, feeling a deep sense of gratitude for the opportunity to experience such intimacy. This was not merely a means to satisfy my own desires; it was an opportunity to pleasure her with the most powerful tool at my disposal - my tongue. Having a massive and very tactile tongue meant that I possessed a unique ability to bring pleasure unlike any other. It was not just about the act itself; it was about the connection formed through the exploration of each other's desires. With every gentle stroke and flick of my tongue, I aimed to unlock new realms of ecstasy for both of us.

Nothing else mattered but the electrifying chemistry between us and the shared pursuit of pleasure. The room became our sanctuary as we delved deeper into a world where boundaries blurred and inhibitions faded away. As I kicked off my shoes and climbed onto the bed, a surge of hope coursed through me. The air was thick with an undeniable tension, fueling the fire that burned within us both. I positioned myself between her legs, slowly inching closer to the centre of her desire. Her breath hitched as my hands trailed up her smooth thighs. Our eyes locked in a primal dance of longing and lust, an unspoken agreement of the pleasures to come.

With each delicate movement, I revelled in the power I held over her. The pretense of our meeting dissolved into a haze of passion and desire, as we surrendered ourselves to the intoxicating rhythm of our bodies. As I gently pulled her panties off, she arched her back, willingly offering herself to me. Without hesitation, my lips met the softness of her inner thighs, leaving a trail of heated kisses in their wake. The taste of her skin lingered on my lips, igniting a hunger that could only be satisfied by indulging in the depths of our carnal desires. Time seemed to stand still as we embarked on a journey filled with ecstasy and pleasure.

We became lost in a world where inhibitions were shed like discarded clothing and every touch was electrifying. The room echoed with our moans and sighs as we explored each other's bodies with an insatiable curiosity. No words were needed; our bodies spoke a language understood only by two souls consumed by their primal instincts. Had I simply stressed wanting to fuck this girl during our exchange of messages, I doubt she would have been so keen to meet. However, in that intimate space between us, where vulnerability merged with raw desire, we discovered something far more profound than mere physical satisfaction. Together, we delved into the depths of our wildest fantasies and embraced our shared yearning for an experience that transcended the ordinary.

The panties were swiftly discarded, landing haphazardly on the floor. With a hunger in my eyes, my mouth descended upon her thigh, tracing a path of tantalizing kisses and licks. As I explored further, my lips discovered the delightful surprise of a tiny mole nestled within the softness of her skin. It added an enticing touch of uniqueness to her already irresistible allure. But it was her pussy that held my utmost attention. Tight and inviting, it beckoned me closer. A neat landing strip of pubic hair acted as a provocative invitation to explore further. Unable to resist, I extended my long tongue and delicately brushed it against her moist and eager lips.

The taste of her arousal coated my tongue, sending shivers down my spine. Eager to please, I continued my journey upwards, seeking out her clitoral hood. As my tongue made contact with this sensitive spot, she gasped in pleasure, signalling her approval. Encircling her clit with precise movements, I savoured each moan and sigh that escaped from her lips. Driven by desire and urgency, I freed myself from the confines of my jeans, revealing the growing feelings within me. With every article of clothing removed, our bodies became more exposed and vulnerable to each other's desires.

While my tongue flicked and circled her sensitive nub, with one hand firmly gripping her thigh, I slid a finger from my other hand into her velvety depths. Her delicate folds eagerly welcomed my digit, allowing it to delve deeper into her tight, sultry core. Savouring the taste of her arousal, I sealed my lips around her throbbing centre, lavishing attention on her pulsating bud. Each flick and tease of my tongue sent shivers of pleasure coursing through her body. Her hips undulated and gyrated against my eager mouth, while my nimble fingers continued their rhythmic exploration within her slick walls. Lost in the intoxicating dance of our bodies, I intensified the pressure of my tongue against her clit, alternating between gentle licks and firm sucks.

The symphony of moans escaping her lips urged me on, driving me to seek new ways to please her. With each thrust of my finger and every flicker of my tongue, I pushed her closer to the edge of ecstasy. The air grew thick with desire as she clutched at the sheets, surrendering herself completely to the pleasure coursing through her veins. Her breath grew ragged and uneven, matching the urgency building between us. In that moment, nothing else mattered but our shared passion and the electric connection that bound us together.

I continued to worship at the altar of her pleasure, skilfully intertwining sensations of pleasure and torment. Every movement purposeful and deliberate as I teased and tormented her senses. She arched against me, craving release as she reached the pinnacle of pleasure that only we could share. As we basked in the afterglow of our carnal union, a satisfied smile played upon both our lips. Our bodies entwined in post-coital bliss, we revelled in the memory of our intimate encounter. A reminder of how deeply we had connected; how we had explored the realms of pleasure and unleashed our innermost desires in a frenzy of passion and lust.

Now her moans were reaching a crescendo, filling the room with the symphony of her pleasure. With each breath, I delved deeper into the art of pussy eating, savouring every taste and texture. My tongue moved with precision and purpose, tracing circles around her firm clit and teasing it with gentle flicks. The intensity grew as I applied more pressure, my mouth engulfing her pussy in a passionate embrace. Her body arched in response, aching for release as I expertly navigated her pleasure centre.

Lost in the moment, I let my instincts guide me, exploring every inch of her sweet pussy. My tongue danced along the folds, exploring the depths of her desire. With each stroke, she surrendered to the ecstasy that coursed through her veins. Her hips rocked in rhythm with my movements, begging for more of my tantalizing touch. As I continued to feast on her forbidden fruit, I could feel the electricity building between us. The connection was primal and raw, our bodies entangled in a dance of passion and lust. Every flick and swirl of my tongue brought us closer to the edge of blissful oblivion. Her moans became cries of ecstasy as I skillfully unleashed wave after wave of pleasure upon her. The world around us faded away as we became lost in our own universe of carnal delights.

Sweat glistened on our bodies as we reveled in the intoxicating mix of desire and satisfaction. In that moment, there was no shame or judgment—only pure unadulterated pleasure. We surrendered ourselves to our primal desires, embracing the freaky and dirty nature of our encounter. And as we reached the pinnacle of ecstasy together, we knew that this experience would forever be etched in our memories as a testament to our insatiable hunger for each other.

Lying on my front on the bed, my face nestled between her thighs that were spread wide apart, I intensified the speed and pressure of my tongue's tantalizing dance. With each flick and swirl, I could feel her arousal mounting, her wetness coating my fingers as they plunged in and out of her pulsating pussy. The sensation of squeezing the inside of her thigh heightened her pleasure, while the rhythm of my fingers inside her matched the tempo of our growing desire.

Her grip tightened on my freshly shaved head, pulling me deeper into her dripping core. Her hips gyrated and thrust against my hungry mouth, driving me to match her fervour with every breathless moan that escaped my lips. The urgency in our movements mirrored the building intensity in the room, as if we were both teetering on the edge of an explosive climax. Though tempted to unleash every trick I had mastered, I held back, savouring this moment; a delicious torment that made us ache for more. Our bodies moved in perfect synchrony, a symphony of passion and pleasure as we explored the depths of our needs. The taste and scent of her drove me wild with a hunger that only grew fiercer with each passing second. I could sense her nearing the precipice of ecstasy, but I wanted to prolong this wicked game just a little longer. The suspense electrified our connection and fuelled our mutual craving for release.

In this intimate dance between tongues and flesh, time seemed to stand still as we delighted in the artistry of pleasure. With every move I made, every stroke and caress, I aimed to push us both further towards that mind-numbing climax that awaited us. Our bodies were locked in an erotic embrace, consumed by an insatiable lust that refused to be tamed. And so we continued our journey towards satisfaction; two souls entwined in a tempestuous storm of passion and desire, ready to surrender to the intoxicating pleasures that lay ahead. She tried to stifle her moans, biting down on her bottom lip as her hips began to spasm uncontrollably. The room was consumed by the sounds of pleasure, a symphony of gasps and sighs that echoed through the walls. Her body quivered with every touch, every stroke sending waves of ecstasy coursing through her veins.

My face was a playground of sensations, taking in the delicious taste and scent of her arousal. With each flick of my tongue, she arched her back, surrendering herself to the pleasure I offered. The wetness of her juices coated my chin, igniting a primal hunger within me. I continued my rhythmic dance on her sensitive flesh, circling, teasing, and pushing against her clit. The intensity grew with each passing moment, as if we were locked in an erotic battle for dominance. Her breathless moans filled the air as she surrendered herself completely to the power of our connection. Determined to push her limits further, I delved deeper into my oral assault. My tongue continued its relentless assault on her clit, flicking and swirling with expert precision. She clung onto me desperately, lost in a haze of pleasure as I became the architect of her wishes.

With each passing second, she drew closer to the edge once again. And just when she thought she couldn't take anymore, I pushed her over that precipice yet again. In that moment of release and surrender, time stood still as our bodies merged in an explosion of pleasure. We were two souls intertwined in a dance of passion and lust, exploring new depths of intimacy together. The night may have been young(ish), but within those moments we created a universe where only our desires mattered. Easing off with the pressure a little, I tilted my head back, allowing my tongue to dart out of my mouth once more. As I extended my long, eager tongue, I relished the opportunity to delve inside her drenched pussy, enjoying the delectable taste of her orgasmic essence.

With each rhythmic thrust of my tongue, I revelled in the sensation of passionately pleasuring this mysterious woman. Gripping her silky thighs firmly, I guided her legs upwards, positioning them against her own chest, granting me unobstructed access to explore every inch of her luscious folds. Taking full control of our intimate encounter, I traced my tongue along the length of her moist slit, navigating between pleasure and desire. Not content with solely indulging in her nectar-filled centre, I ventured further down to caress the delicate contours of her puckered entrance, teasing it with gentle flicks before plunging my tongue into the tightness of her forbidden territory.

I enjoy exploring a woman's body, and that includes indulging in some kinky play. While I don't mind licking a girl's ass, I find that it's best experienced alongside pleasuring her pussy. It's all about finding the perfect balance of sensations and driving her wild with pleasure. The ass is an incredibly sensitive area, and if she's into it, it can bring a whole new level of ecstasy. As I continued to pleasure her, my tongue expertly danced between her clit and her tight little hole. Each flick and swirl of my tongue brought her closer to the edge, causing wave after wave of intense orgasms to wash over her. With her legs pulled back towards her chest, I had easy access to finger her dripping wet pussy, intensifying each orgasm that wracked through her body.

I don't know about other guys, but when I'm indulging in the art of cunnilingus, my focus is unwavering. I immerse myself completely, entering a state of heightened awareness that borders on the ethereal. As I caress and explore with my tongue, my eyes may even surrender to the pleasure, shutting out the distractions of the world. It's as if I can feel every contour and texture of the luscious pussy before me, painting a vivid picture in my mind. This transcendental experience is what sets me apart; it's why I excel at this intimate act, excelling beyond measure. The truth is, I derive immense satisfaction from it, pouring every ounce of energy into this sensual pursuit. Especially in moments of intense passion, where boundaries are shattered and inhibitions unravel, becomes more than a mere desire—it becomes my ultimate fetish.

Over the course of the next few hours, her clit was lavished with attention. It was a tantalizing symphony of pleasure as my tongue danced across its sensitive bud, sending waves of ecstasy coursing through her body. I took in the delicious taste of her arousal, appreciating every drop that escaped her quivering lips. Her moans filled the room, urging me on to explore her deepest desires. As I continued to feast upon her nectar, my fingers joined in the erotic dance. They slid effortlessly inside her, exploring the wetness and tightness that enveloped them. With each thrust, she gasped and writhed beneath me, lost in a sea of carnal bliss. Unable to resist any longer, I positioned myself between her legs and plunged deep into her warmth. Her walls clenched around me hungrily, welcoming my intrusion with open arms. The rhythm intensified as our bodies moved as one, a primal connection forged in the fires of passion.

Her hands clawed at my back, leaving red marks in their wake, a testament to the intensity of our desire. Sweat glistened on our skin as we pushed each other further towards the edge of ecstasy. In this moment, there were no limits or boundaries; only pure pleasure and unadulterated lust. Positions swapped and she sat on my face, her groin pressing against my eager mouth as my hand continued to explore her body. The taste of her arousal lingered on my tongue as I savoured every moment of our intimate connection. With each flick of my tongue, I could feel her body tremble with pleasure, her moans filling the room.

As the night progressed, we delved deeper into our desires, pushing boundaries and exploring new sensations. Her hips gyrated against my face, the wetness between her legs coating my lips and chin. I understood the power she granted me as I pleasured her relentlessly. The intensity of our encounter grew with each passing moment, igniting a fire within us that seemed impossible to extinguish. The room echoed with the symphony of our pleasure, a symphony composed of gasps, moans, and whispered profanities. We were lost in each other's touch, consumed by an insatiable hunger for more. Time ceased to exist as we indulged in the depths of our desires.

Eventually, exhaustion overcame us both, but not before we had exhausted every ounce of pleasure from one another. As we drifted off to sleep in each other's arms, sated and content, I knew that this night would forever remain etched in my mind as a testament to the power of unbridled desire and unapologetic exploration. Just a few hours later my alarm went off reminding me that I still had a day's work to do. However, the memory of the previous night's encounter lingered in my mind, making it impossible to focus on anything else. The sensation of indulging in dirty, freaky sex with a stranger was still fresh on my skin, igniting a desire for more. Ignoring my responsibilities, I set another alarm on my phone and surrendered to the temptation of sleep once again.

As I drifted back into slumber, I couldn't help but recall the taste of her as I devoured her pussy with enthusiasm. The thought alone sent shivers down my spine, arousing a primal hunger within me. Awakening to the sound of my second alarm, reality slowly seeped back into my consciousness. With a raspy voice that hinted at the debauchery from the night before, I mustered up the courage to call in sick to work. By ten in the morning, both she and I had fully awakened from our blissful slumber. We lay there together, trying to comprehend the intensity and unexpectedness of our encounter. It was as if fate had conspired to bring us together for that wild night of passionate pleasure. The air still crackled with an undeniable chemistry between us, leaving us both craving more of each other's touch.

Though responsibilities called and obligations loomed over us like dark clouds, we couldn't help but indulge in fantasies of what could transpire if we were to meet again. The memory of her luscious body intertwined with mine fueled a fire within me that burned hot and wild. In that moment, work seemed insignificant compared to the raw connection we had discovered. As I laid there beside her, contemplating whether to succumb once more or face reality head-on, one thing became clear - this encounter had forever changed me. It was a reminder that life is meant to be lived passionately, exploring the depths of our desires without shame or restraint. And for that, I would forever cherish the memory of that freaky, nasty night of pleasure.

We both agreed that this was a 'no strings' encounter and said our goodbyes. I left her some cash to cover the hotel, a small token of appreciation for the wild night we had shared. As I handed it to her, a mischievous smile played on her lips, hinting at the unforgettable pleasure we had indulged in. She whispered her gratitude, acknowledging the intense passion that had consumed us throughout the night. And in return, I expressed my sincere thanks for the privilege of savoring every delicious moment of tasting her sweet nectar. Our minds were still reeling from the electrifying connection we had experienced, leaving an insatiable hunger for more passionate encounters in our wake. We parted ways with a lingering desire, knowing that we had set the bar high for future escapades. The memory of our explicit rendezvous would forever fuel our fantasies, igniting flames of desire whenever we recalled those moments of unadulterated pleasure.

Sploshing

I opened that anus up wide like a bucket,
Stuck my fist up in her, and played with that ass like a puppet.
No doubt her ass was big, But I explored every curve, every
jiggle, every digit.
With each touch and caress, the pleasure grew,
And the heat between us ignited.

~

In the realm of passion and desire,
We danced to the rhythm of our bodies' fire.
Exploring new depths, we pushed the boundaries of lust,
As we surrendered ourselves to an insatiable thrust.
Together we soared, reaching heights never before known,
In this intimate dance where pleasure was our throne.

Six

Tom

To be honest, I don't really care if anyone judges me or talks shit. I just want to make it clear that I'm not ashamed of my sexual preferences; they're just simply on the freakier side. So, let me get straight to the point because, truth be told, I'm getting all hot and bothered just thinking about this story. It all began when I was young and realized that I had a strong affinity for the booty. I mean, everything about it drove me wild - from its visual appeal to the way it felt and even its taste.

As I grew older, my passion for ass-eating only intensified. The way a perfectly shaped posterior would entice me was beyond comprehension. Every time my tongue made contact with those luscious cheeks, an indescribable pleasure surged through my body. People may find it dirty or nasty, but for me, it was pure ecstasy. Now, before you judge or label me as some kind of pervert, under-stand that these desires are nothing more than a part of who I am. And to be honest, exploring this aspect of my sexuality has brought me immense satisfaction and pleasure. So why should I feel ashamed? After all, what happens behind closed doors is nobody's business but mine.

So, I decided to do a bit of an experiment, and because I had a girlfriend who was just as adventurous as me, I thought 'why not?' You know, we were both into exploring our wild side. That day is still etched in my memory like it happened yesterday. I headed to McDonald's and grabbed a six-piece nuggets meal with a side of fries and a sinful vanilla milkshake. The rush was building up inside me as I couldn't wait to get home and dive into my little project. As soon as I walked through the door, I called out for Sarah to join me downstairs. With a mischievous smile on my face, I couldn't help but feel excited about what was to come. We were about to push the boundaries of pleasure and test our limits in ways we never had before. As I arrived home, I yelled for Sarah to come downstairs.

"I'm coming, motherfucker, don't rush me," she yelled back with a hint of playfulness in her voice.

Excitement coursed through my veins as I quickly stripped off my clothes, leaving me standing in the living room completely naked. The thought of what was to come fueled my desire, making me even more eager for my girlfriend's arrival. Minutes seemed like an eternity as I stood there, my heart pounding with nervousness. Finally, the sound of footsteps echoed through the hallway, growing louder with each passing second. My gaze fixated on the doorway as she entered, clad only in a seductive towel that hugged her curves perfectly. The sight of her made my pulse race and thoughts of devouring her consumed my mind. Lust hung heavy in the air as our eyes locked, a silent understanding passing between us. We both knew that tonight was going to be one filled with intense passion and pleasure.

Without uttering a single word, we closed the distance between us. Our bodies collided in a frenzy of longing and desire. The taste of her lips was intoxicating as our tongues danced together in a passionate tango. Exploring every inch of each other's bodies became our sole mission, leaving no stone unturned. In this moment, nothing else mattered except the raw and primal connection we shared. We embraced our freaky side, indulging in dirty sex that pushed the boundaries of pleasure.

"Are you ready to try this, baby?" I asked with a mischievous grin on my face.

"Well yes, Tom, I even prepared myself for you," she replied.

"Well then, let's dive right into the depths of pleasure," I responded, my voice laced with excitement.

As she reclined on the sofa, I began to explore her body with fervent kisses, starting from her lips and trailing down to every inch of her skin. I understood that while I may not have been in the mood for all the sweet nothings, she craved them like a drug, and denying her would only hinder our shared experience. With an open mind and a lustful spirit, I embraced the art of seduction as our tongues intertwined in a passionate dance. Trying to maintain the unpredictable pace, I explored her stomach with eager kisses, my lips tracing a tantalizing path downwards. As I ventured below her umbilicus, I could feel the eagerness building within me, craving more than just a quick rendezvous with her vulva. No, my desires were fixated on something naughtier, something that would set my senses ablaze. The thought of delving into that forbidden territory was enough to make my heart race and my palms sweat.

Undeterred by any reservations she may have had, I continued my descent, my tongue now gliding along her pubic bone. Her response was undeniable as she began to lose herself in the moment, her hands exploring every inch of her body with an urgency that matched my own. With each passing second, the air grew thicker with desire and the room seemed to pulse with an electric energy. There was an unspoken understanding between us, a shared craving for something beyond the ordinary. And as she tilted her head back in ecstasy, I knew that we were about to embark on a journey unlike any other. In that moment, there was no room for hesitation or inhibition; only raw passion driving us forward.

It was a moment of pure bliss and unadulterated ecstasy; a moment where time stood still and all that mattered was the intoxicating connection between two souls lost in their own carnal desires. I continued my tantalizing exploration, my tongue delving deeper into her wetness. The taste of her arousal filled my mouth, mixing with the lingering flavour of her ass. With each lick and flick, I could feel her body arching in pleasure beneath me. Her moans grew louder as I skilfully conniver between her thighs, teasing and stimulating every inch of her intimate areas.

With each gentle thrust of my tongue into her tight asshole, she moaned with a mix of surprise and delight. Her hips bucked against me, urging me to go deeper. I obliged, pushing the boundaries of pleasure as I continued my relentless assault. The taste of her forbidden fruit lingered on my lips as we kissed passionately, sharing the intimate flavours that drove us both wild. Our bodies moved in perfect synchronization as we reached new heights of ecstasy together. It was a raw and primal connection that left us breathless and hungry for more. As our bodies finally succumbed to exhaustion, we lay tangled in each other's arms, basking in the afterglow of our uninhibited passion.

"I taste so good, baby," she moaned, her voice dripping with desire.

I smirked, my mind filled with naughty thoughts.

"Damn right, your ass taste like a strawberry dove soap, baby girl." The words rolled off my tongue in a seductive whisper.

With a mischievous grin, I shifted my focus downwards, exploring the depths of her pleasure. Sliding two fingers inside of her, I felt her walls clench around me, a delicious sensation that fuelled my excitement. Drawing her closer to me, I flicked my tongue against her swollen clit, savouring the taste of her arousal. The way she squirmed and moaned only intensified my hunger for her. Her body trembled beneath me as I continued to suck and nibble on her sensitive nub. Her hands desperately grasped at the sheets as waves of ecstasy washed over her. My relentless ministrations brought her to the edge of blissful surrender. She writhed uncontrollably, yearning for release while I expertly teased and pleased her.

Then, I felt a surge of sensuality engulf me. With my tongue still pleasuring her, I couldn't resist exploring further. I gently introduced two fingers into the depths of her ass, and in response, she pressed her eager womanhood against my face, as if urging me to take her from behind with all my might. Gradually, I moved her onto her stomach, ensuring not to release her throbbing clit from the grip of my mouth. The rhythm intensified as I continued thrusting my fingers into her tight ass, one after another, twisting and penetrating like it was our last encounter with such intimate anal pleasure. She moaned for more as I released my fingers from her wet ass and teasingly placed them into her waiting mouth. With an insatiable hunger, she eagerly sucked on them, appreciating the taste of her own intoxicating flavour. Feeling the intensity of her desire growing, she pleaded with a wild passion in her eyes.

"I need you to slide your fingers back inside me, deeper and harder."

Unable to resist her pleas, I thrust three fingers deep into the depths of her throbbing core, feeling her walls tighten around them. Slowly, I withdrew my fingers and offered them to her again, watching as she greedily accepted them between parted lips. Lost in a haze of ecstasy and craving more, she whispered in a husky voice.

"I want you to fuck my ass tonight baby. Take me to places I've never been before."

Driven by an unquenchable lust, I honoured her command without hesitation. Gently removing my fingers from her mouth, I positioned myself behind her, ready to fulfil her darkest needs.

As I prepared to enter the forbidden territory of her tight ass, she arched her back and moaned uncontrollably. With each thrust, we delved deeper into a realm of pleasure that was both exhilarating and taboo. In that moment of blissful surrender, our bodies tangled in a symphony of carnal delight. We embraced our inner freaks and unleashed our wildest passions upon each other's willing souls. As I spread her legs wide on the sofa, I slowly slid my cock into her tight asshole.

"Oh, baby, that feels so good," she moaned.

I increased the pressure, and her ass stretched to accommodate my thick shaft. The sensation was mind-blowing, just as it always was. She writhed on the couch, creating an array of seductive expressions that only fuelled my needs for her. With my head thrown back, I intensified the rhythm, pounding her ass with every thrust. Her moans grew louder with each powerful stroke, our bodies locked in a passionate dance of pleasure.

Sweat glistened on our skin as we lost ourselves in the throes of ecstasy. I relished in the sounds of our bodies colliding, the erotic symphony of flesh meeting flesh. Every thrust sent waves of pleasure coursing through me, urging me to delve deeper into her forbidden depths. I was on the verge of releasing my load inside her tight ass, but my primal instincts kicked in. It was too early, and there was something else I desired. Ignoring any potential consequences, I resolved to satisfy my deepest fantasy, even if it meant defying divine intervention.

Switching into a dominant mindset, I commanded her attention. With her head tilted to the side, she eagerly observed as I focused my energy. Gently withdrawing my throbbing member from her anus, I formed my hand into a tight fist and cautiously inserted my entire right wrist into her waiting cavity. The sensation caused her to emit a guttural moan, resembling the desperate cry of a famished animal. Every thrust of my hand unleashed a wave of pleasure and pain that merged into an intoxicating blend. The look in her eyes revealed her surrender to the twisted passion that consumed us both. We were lost in a realm where boundaries blurred and inhibitions ceased to exist.

"Ahhhhhhh, shit, oh my God, Jesus Christ baby, wow, I can't breathe," she screamed in a mix of pleasure and pain.

Her cries only fuelled my desire as I intensified the thrust of my hand inside her ass. The room was filled with the sounds of her moans and the wet slapping noise as my hand moved in and out. Her body trembled under my touch, aching for more as I continued to stretch her open. With each deep penetration, I could feel her walls tightening around my wrist, embracing the invading sensation. The feeling of power surged through me as I pushed deeper and deeper into her. The rhythm became almost hypnotic as I pulled my fist out slowly, savouring the sight of her gaping hole, before plunging it back in forcefully. Her body convulsed with pleasure mixed with pain, unable to resist the sinful pleasure that coursed through her veins.

Time seemed to blur as we lost ourselves in this taboo act of pleasure. Her cries grew louder, matching the intensity of each thrust. Every movement was met with a wave of ecstasy that sent shivers down our spines. As we reached the peak of our passion, she arched her back and let out a primal scream that echoed through the room. The release was overwhelming, leaving us breathless and satisfied. At one point, I felt a surge of anticipation as my hands explored the depths within her. The intensity of our connection was overwhelming, making me yearn for even more intimate sensations. Moments later, a shiver ran through my body as I felt my arousal reaching its peak, begging to be released. With a sudden burst of desire, I withdrew my hands and guided myself into her enticing rear entrance. The sensation was unlike anything I had ever experienced before, as if every nerve in my body had been awakened. In mere seconds, the powerful climax consumed me, and I unleashed all my passion deep inside her tight and inviting asshole. The pleasure continued to course through us both as I indulged in the forbidden act for a few glorious minutes, savouring every moment of our shared ecstasy.

Now this was where my experiment started. Wanting to ensure that none of the juice would leak out, I carefully positioned my girlfriend upside down, her legs pointed towards the ceiling, effectively sealing her anus and preventing any cum from escaping. With anticipation, I reached for the box of chicken nuggets and fries that I had bought from McDonald's earlier. Slowly and meticulously, I dipped each nugget into her inviting ass, relishing in the naughtiness of the act. As I savoured the flavours of the fast food and my own unique dip sauce, a surge of excitement coursed through me. The combination of the forbidden pleasure and the familiar taste created an unmatched sensory experience. This unconventional experiment pushed boundaries and allowed us to explore new heights of pleasure together. It was a freaky encounter that awakened our desires and brought us closer than ever before.

It didn't taste too bad, to be honest. In fact, if you asked me, my cum tasted absolutely amazing. After relishing a few of the nuggets, I decided to take things a step further. I dipped the last one in her tight little anus and delicately placed it in her awaiting mouth. With a mischievous grin on my face, I couldn't help but ask.

"How does that naughty treat taste, baby?" She struggled to maintain her balance as her body contorted into various positions.

She managed to respond amidst the pleasure.

"Well, the nuggets are a little cold, but surprisingly delicious, your sauce is amazing baby."

Emboldened by her response, I continued to explore new depths of pleasure. One by one, I dipped my fries into her eager orifice. Each bite was more delectable than the last, leaving me craving for more. The combination of flavours and sensations was unlike anything I had ever experienced before. It was an indulgence that pushed the boundaries of conventional pleasure. As we revelled in our freaky escapade, it became clear that there was no limit to our desires. In that moment, we embraced our primal instincts and let go of all inhibitions. We were unapologetically filthy and nasty in our pursuit of ecstasy. The taste of forbidden pleasure lingered on our tongues as we delved deeper into the depths of our desires. After experiencing the unique combination of flavours from my creamy cum and the vanilla milkshake, I couldn't help but feel a surge of excitement running through me. The intense satisfaction from my indulgence with nuggets and fries had left me craving for more. As the thirst lingered, I noticed her body glistening, beckoning me to explore further. With a mischievous grin, I retrieved my vanilla milkshake from the floor and decided to take our pleasure to new heights.

Carefully removing the lid, I poured the velvety liquid into the depths of her waiting anus. The sensation was electrifying, as if we were embarking on an uncharted journey of pleasure and desire. The straw found its place inside her, allowing me to savour every drop of the tantalizing mixture we had created together. Each sip sent waves of ecstasy rippling through both our bodies. As our passion reached its crescendo, I couldn't resist tasting her lips once more, allowing our tongues to dance in a fervent embrace. With an intoxicating blend of my cum and the remaining vanilla milkshake still lingering in my mouth, I released it all into her eager mouth. She eagerly swallowed, welcoming the merging flavours as they cascaded down her throat. About two minutes later, she stood up, her body glistening with sweat. The air crackled with an electric energy as she slowly lowered herself, laying down flat on the ground. I watched, my eyes filled with desire, as she beckoned me to join her in this forbidden act.

With every inch of my being pulsating with excitement, I moved closer, ensuring that I was the one who would catch the remnants of our passion. I positioned myself strategically, ready to taste the essence of our intimate connection. As our bodies intertwined in a dance of pleasure and ecstasy, I couldn't help but marvel at how this experiment had brought us to new heights of pleasure. It was a thrilling exploration of our desires and boundaries, leaving no stone unturned in our quest for ultimate satisfaction. While our paths may have diverged since that unforgettable encounter, the memory lingers like a tantalizing secret. She will forever remain the epitome of sensuality and allure; a reminder of the intense moments we shared. This experience awakened within me a hunger for more unconventional pleasures. It ignited a fire within me, pushing me to explore the boundaries of pleasure and indulge in my deepest fantasies. Sex became my playground, where experimentation and indulgence knew no bounds.

And so, my journey continues down this path of sensual discovery. Each encounter is an opportunity to delve deeper into the realms of pleasure and intimacy. With every new experience comes another chapter in my story; a testament to the power that lies within exploring our most primal desires. In this world where passion reigns supreme, where taboos are embraced rather than shunned, I have found liberation. Through the fusion of sex and food, I have discovered an endless wellspring of pleasure waiting to be explored. And trust me when I say there is so much more left untold; stories that will leave you breathless and craving for more.

Coprophilia

So, you had shit coming out of your anus?
Y'all are really out here trying to be famous,
Right in her mouth, yet you were aimless,
But she wanted it so, you could always be blameless.

~

In the pursuit of fame, y'all went to extremes,
Pushing boundaries and breaking social norms it seems,
Though unconventional, it fuelled your dreams,
To stand out from the crowd, and make a scene.

~

With unapologetic audacity, you took your chance,
Leaving a lasting impression with every glance,
Unafraid to provoke or challenge the dance,
Your quest for fame became a wild romance.

~

Amidst the chaos and controversy that ensued,
You remained unfazed, your image shrewd,
For in her desires, you found solace and food,
Aiming for notoriety, emotions subdued.

Seven

Adam

As I towered above her, my throbbing member nestled in the palm of my hand, she lay sprawled on the cold ground, her supple flesh exposed for my eyes to feast upon. Her voluptuous bosom, adorned with double-D breasts, beckoned me closer, their firmness aching to be caressed. I fixated my gaze upon her naked form, her mouth agape, ready for the pleasure that was about to consume her. With each stroke of my engorged cock, I sought to establish a connection through our locked eyes, but she resisted my advances, writhing sensually across the floor.

She embodied everything that was forbidden and alluring - my filthy little enchantress. Our paths had converged on a twisted platform of desire and deviance years ago when we rendezvoused on an unconventional dating site dedicated solely to exploring depraved fantasies. Behind closed doors, we unleashed our darkest desires without fear of judgment or inhibition. The walls of our secret sanctuary witnessed acts that would make the faint-hearted shudder; pleasures that ventured into uncharted territories of eroticism and carnal satisfaction.

She was happy being my submissive plaything, surrendering herself completely to my insatiable appetite for perversion. Together we delved into realms where conventional boundaries were obliterated and replaced by a symphony of moans and cries echoing through the night. In her embrace, I found solace from a world that feigned innocence while secretly craving the same wicked pleasures we indulged in. We were two souls bound by a shared hunger for adventure beyond societal norms - a tempestuous duo destined to explore the realms of freaky passion and unapologetic lust. No matter how much time passes or how distant we may become, she will forever remain etched in the deepest recesses of my mind as the embodiment of all things naughty and tantalizing. Our liaison may have been clandestine, but the memories we crafted together will forever burn bright in the depths of my depraved thirst.

See, I have always had these certain fetishes that needed to be taken care of, and she was the only one who was willing to succumb to my every need. It's not something I openly discuss with others, but behind closed doors, we indulged in our freaky preferences. I had a seemingly normal life with a wife, two kids, and a dog - the perfect picture of a family man. However, deep down, I craved something more intense and prohibited. That's when she entered my life, like a seductive temptress who understood my darkest secrets. When we first met, I never would have guessed that she harboured the same dirty secrets as me. She appeared innocent and sweet - a thirty-year-old girl with an aura of naivety. Little did anyone know the depths of her sexual appetite. And there I was, hitting fifty but still drawn to the young ones. It seemed like fate had brought us together - two souls craving forbidden pleasures.

Our encounters were nothing short of electrifying. From coprophilia to other explicit acts that some might consider nasty or even disgusting, we were happy in our shared perversions. In those moments, age and societal expectations were irrelevant. We found solace in each other's arms, free from judgment or shame. Together, we created our own world where anything was possible - a world where our cravings for dirty sex were fulfilled without hesitation.

She became my partner in crime, my confidante in this secret underworld of desires. We celebrated our mutual understanding and unleashed our fantasies upon each other with uninhibited passion. Our connection went beyond physical gratification; it was an exploration of our deepest selves. So yes, I may have had a conventional facade - a devoted husband and father by day. But when the night fell and the bedroom door closed, I delved into a world of ecstasy with her. Our encounters were an escape from societal norms, a journey into the depths of our freaky and nasty desires. And together, we discovered a level of satisfaction that surpassed anything I had ever known before. The first time we laid eyes on each other, I whisked her away to a fancy restaurant in the vibrant west end. As we sat down and ordered our meal, the conversation flowed effortlessly between us. We delved deep into topics that most people would shy away from, unafraid to explore the complexities of our cravings. There was no room for pretense or beating around the bush; we were both clear about what we craved. Despite the age difference, which some might consider scandalous, our connection was undeniable.

Over dinner, our words danced with an intoxicating mix of intellect and raw passion. We bared our souls to one another, sharing secrets and fantasies that had long been hidden away. The allure of the forbidden only heightened our needs. I didn't hold back as I revealed my truth: I had a wife and two children waiting for me at home. It was a confession that could have shattered our connection, but she surprised me by handling it with grace. She understood that there were certain things my wife couldn't provide, needs that only she could consummate. In those moments together, boundaries blurred and inhibitions faded away. Our encounters became increasingly intense as we ventured into uncharted territories of pleasure. Our connection was more than just physical; it was a meeting of minds and souls equally drawn to the unconventional.

As we indulged in each other's company, our passion grew wilder and more untamed. We embraced the freaky and embraced the nasty - knowing that within this realm of dirty sex lay an authenticity that few dared to embrace. You see, I was one of those men who entered into marriage solely to appease my affluent parents. I showered my wife with everything she desired, but little consideration was given to my own needs and emotions. It seemed that nobody truly cared about the man's perspective in a relationship. This realization prompted me to seek out someone who would understand my inner demons, which is exactly what she did.

As I gazed upon her delicate figure, a surge of arousal coursed through me. My erection grew firm and pulsating, eager to unleash its carnal desires upon her. She responded with moans and groans of pleasure, her body becoming a canvas for our most intimate passions. The intensity of our connection intensified as we explored the depths of our darkest fantasies. I guess that was the jolt of excitement I needed, because in that very moment, a surge of desire coursed through me. She had ignited a fire within, and I couldn't resist her passionate plea.

"Give it to me, daddy," she cried out, her voice filled with longing.

The raw intensity of her words sent shivers down my spine. Without hesitation, I took control, embracing the carnal desire that consumed us both. Our bodies tangled together in a frenzy of lust and need. Her skin glistened with sweat as our movements grew more intense. We surrendered to our darkest desires, exploring every taboo possibility. It was like dancing on the edge of sanity, losing ourselves in the intoxicating haze of ecstasy. In the midst of this fiery passion, she whispered words that fueled my desire even further.

"I want you now," she pleaded, her voice dripping with desperation.

The intensity of her longing only served to heighten my own primal urges. I let out a groan as I finished urinating, shaking off the last drops. Finally, it was time. That big lunch I had eaten earlier was ready to make its grand exit.

"Give it to me, daddy," she moaned eagerly. "I'm ready for all of you. I'll do whatever you want, baby. I love you so much." She went on, expressing her love and enthusiasm for consuming my waste.

"I hope you had something delicious today, baby. Did you have some chocolate ice cream for dessert? Tell me what you ate," she purred in a seductive voice, anticipating the taste of my bowel movement.

"Well, you're about to find out," I responded with a mischievous grin as I positioned myself above her face.

With my legs spread wide open, the anticipation of indulging in our freaky desires filled the room. As my body hovered over hers, I could feel the electricity pulsating through every inch of my being. This act, this forbidden pleasure, was a manifestation of our unapologetic nastiness and raw passion. The scent in the air heightened the intensity, fueling our lustful desires even more. With each release, we experienced a liberation unlike any other; a freedom that only comes from embracing one's true desires without judgement or shame. It was in these moments that we found solace, where our dirty sex became an art form - an expression of love untamed by societal expectations.

It came fluctuating out of my ass as I held my Gluteus Medius in my hands. Her mouth still wide open, eagerly awaiting the next taste of my taboo desires. The thrill of indulging in such a freaky act made me shiver, heightening the intensity of the moment. As she swallowed my faeces, her tongue grazed against it, savoring the dirty pleasure that we both craved. The sensation of her chewing and touching it ignited a fire within me, driving me to produce even bigger faeces. I had deliberately chosen a meal that would expedite the process, but now I felt a slight obstruction in my anus. With determination, I pushed through the resistance and forced my faeces out, desperate to fulfill both our desires. However, in my eagerness, a loud fart escaped me, creating an unexpected explosion of nastiness that only added to the perverse excitement we shared.

"For fuck sake baby, did you drink that milk again? You know that you're lactose intolerant, damn," she whispered.

This chick was well aware of my lactose intolerance and yet I still couldn't resist the temptation to drink that damn milk.

"I'm sorry, baby, please forgive me," I pleaded, hoping she would have some mercy this time.

But instead of showing any remorse, she smirked.

"Well, I can't just sit here and have you farting all over my face now can I!?"

Her words hit me like a slap in the face. Did she really think I enjoyed dealing with the aftermath of dairy consumption? It was embarrassing and downright nasty. Unable to argue with her logic, I reluctantly agreed to finish off in the toilet before we proceeded to have our freaky shower session. It wasn't exactly the romantic encounter I had envisioned, but desperate times called for desperate measures. As I struggled to stand up from the ground, cursing that motherfucking dairy under my breath, I couldn't help but wonder why I put myself through this. Was the pleasure worth the pain? But then again, there was something undeniably thrilling about indulging in forbidden pleasures. Maybe it was the thrill of breaking societal norms or maybe it was just our own dirty little secret. Either way, it kept us coming back for more, no matter how much it fucked up our day.

As she rinsed away the remnants of our wild escapade in the steam-filled shower, my urge to relieve myself vanished. Instead, I eagerly joined her under the cascading water, feeling a renewed sense of desire coursing through my veins. It seemed that the previous tension had dissipated, replaced by an intoxicating air of intimacy. Without hesitation, she dropped to her knees, her eyes locked with mine as she engulfed my throbbing member in her warm mouth. The sensation was electrifying as her skilled tongue danced and teased, driving me to the brink of ecstasy. In that moment, I realized just how deeply I adored this woman; her uninhibited nature was a revelation.

Hours later, when I finally arrived home and shed the trappings of daily life at the door, I was greeted by the sight of my wife standing in the kitchen with a mischievous grin on her face. Her embrace enveloped me in warmth and familiarity, erasing any remnants of mundane existence from my mind. Our children scampered behind her, their innocent laughter filling our home with joy and delight.

"Hey, honey," she said as she greeted me with a warm embrace. The kids then rushed over, their excitement palpable as they embraced me tightly.

"Daddy, we've been waiting for you all day," my daughter exclaimed, her voice filled with joy. "We missed you so much!"

"I missed you too, sweetheart," I replied, my heart swelling with love for my family.

Suddenly, my son piped up with a curious expression on his face.

"Daddy, why do you smell funny?" he asked innocently.

Caught off guard, I glanced at my wife who raised an eyebrow in amusement.

"Oh well," I chuckled nervously, trying to come up with a suitable response.

"I must have had an encounter with a skunk on my way home."

Laughter filled the air as we made our way into the kitchen, ready to share stories of our day and enjoy a delicious meal together. It was these simple moments that reminded me of how lucky I was to have such a loving and playful family, but even luckier to have her.

Eleven Inch Desire

Oh yes, he was my boyfriend's friend,
The sex was so good, I had to make amends.

~

No, I did not plan for this twist,
But his touch left me in a state of bliss.

~

His hands roamed my body with such finesse,
Leaving me breathless and unable to confess.

~

I wanted to resist, but he ignited a fire,
A desire that consumed me, taking me higher.

~

In the darkness of night, our bodies entwined,
Passion and pleasure intertwined.

~

Oh yes, he was my boyfriend's friend,
But in those moments, the world would suspend.

Eight

Mary

We were partying in my dorm room, the music blaring and the sweet smell of cannabis filling the air. The atmosphere was electric, fired by laughter and the shared indulgence of drugs. As we passed around joints and took hits from a makeshift bong, our inhibitions melted away. The room was alive with conversation and flirtatious glances, everyone basking in the blissful haze of intoxication. But amidst the chaos and euphoria, I couldn't help but feel a tinge of vulnerability creeping in. The coke coursing through my veins had taken its toll, leaving me feeling weak and unsteady. I gazed at my boyfriend Keith, his eyes glazed over with a mixture of pleasure and mischief. In a voice laced with desperation, I whispered to him,

"I'm fucked, baby."

A mischievous grin spread across his face as he responded,

"I know," he giggled, "me too."

We both exchanged knowing smiles, a shared understanding of our desires. Despite the fact that I was well aware I had already indulged in an excessive amount of coke, my craving for another line persisted. The allure of surrendering to a state of blissful oblivion fuelled my desire. Determined to reach that point, I rose from my seat and knelt beside the small table in my room. With deliberate precision, I carefully lined up a fresh line of the white powder and eagerly inhaled it. As I brushed off my nose, I returned to where my boyfriend patiently awaited me. Settling back down beside him, he pulled me close and his hands ventured towards my breasts. Curiosity tinged with excitement filled the air as I gazed at him, a playful smile gracing my lips.

"What do you think you're doing?" I playfully questioned him.

A mischievous glint sparkled in his eyes as he pleaded.

"Let's make love right here, baby."

Intoxicated by both substances and desire, a tipsy giggle escaped my lips as he leaned in to kiss me.

"You're absolutely insane," I responded, a hint of disbelief lacing my voice, even as I eagerly reciprocated his passion by plunging my tongue into his mouth.

We sat there and kissed for a few minutes. My shirt was suddenly off, but I didn't mind. My head was spinning with anticipation, and my body was craving to be touched. A few moments later, my bra was ripped off, exposing my bare nipples. As I looked up at him, he began nibbling on them while Mark and Davina watched in shock.

"Are you guys really having sex right now?" asked Mark, breaking the silence.

But Keith, my boyfriend, paid no attention as he continued sucking on my breasts. Davina couldn't believe her eyes and began licking her lips as if she wanted to join in. She got up from her spot and walked over to us, almost as if we were in a movie. Without hesitation, she pushed Keith aside and started kissing him passionately. I was in disbelief watching this unfold before me.

"Did this girl just kiss my boyfriend?"

I thought to myself, feeling a mix of anger and confusion. But they were both clearly enjoying themselves. Even though I was high as a kite, I wasn't stupid. Meanwhile, Davina's actions only increased my curiosity. Davina suddenly stopped and gazed at me, her eyes burning with lust. She slowly walked over and knelt by my side, her fingers trailing lightly down my body. A soft sigh escaped my lips as she started kissing my stomach, her tongue exploring every inch of my skin until it reached my breast. I couldn't help but gasp as she teased and caressed me, sending shivers of pleasure through my body.

Meanwhile, Keith wasted no time in opening my jeans and sliding them off, his intense gaze fixed on me the whole time. His lips met the sensitive skin of my inner thighs, leaving a trail of hot kisses as he made his way to my center. With expert skill, he used his tongue to gently remove my panties before delving between my legs. My breath caught in my throat as his warm tongue danced over me, igniting a fire within me that I couldn't ignore. And just when I thought it couldn't get any better, Davina quickly took off her shirt, revealing her readiness for me. My heart raced as Keith spread my legs open wide, his lips still kissing and nibbling on my sweet spot while his fingers plunged deep inside me.

He then opened me up even wider so he could suck on my clit aggressively, sending bolts of electricity through every nerve in my body. I moaned in ecstasy, unable to believe that this was actually happening. It felt like a scene from a steamy movie, with me as the star attraction. As Davina used her skilled tongue to bring me to climax multiple times, Keith walked over to her and roughly penetrated her with his impressive nine-inch dick. The room was filled with the sounds of our passionate moans and cries, almost akin to a live porn show being directed by Mark who couldn't resist capturing it all on his phone.

The intensity of our shared pleasure only grew as we explored each other's bodies, our desires and lust driving us to new heights of ecstasy. It was a night I would never forget, filled with passion, pleasure, and the uninhibited pursuit of our deepest desires. The intimate setting of two stunning women and one man engaged in passionate acts was enough to make anyone's heart race. Even someone who identified as gay would have felt an urge to join in on the filming. But this particular guy seemed more than just open-minded - he was eager and excited to participate. I watched as he stripped down, revealing his toned body and impressive endowment. He approached me with confidence, standing over me with his cock in hand. My eyes were immediately drawn to its length and girth, and I couldn't resist reaching out for it eagerly, like a child yearning for candy.

"Come here," I whispered, my voice low and sultry.

I took hold of his massive eleven-inch dick, attempting to fit it into my mouth. But it proved too large for me to handle; there was no way I was going to be outdone by this man. With determination, I pushed Davina away from me as she continued to be ravaged by Keith - my ex-boyfriend. And in that moment, he truly was an ex, as he had completely forgotten about my existence; but I didn't care. Mark's dick was going to be mine to conquer. He lifted me up against the wall and began pleasuring me in a way that I had never experienced before. His tongue teased and explored every inch of my dripping pussy, consuming me with unbridled desire. Unlike most men who spit or wipe away their partner's arousal during oral sex, Mark devoured every last drop with insatiable hunger. He left me speechless and utterly satisfied.

In that moment of pure ecstasy, I couldn't help but think to myself.

"If only I had known about Mark's incredible skills earlier, perhaps I would have chosen him instead of Keith."

The thought only added to my pleasure and pushed my desire for more of Mark's expert touch. Mark gently placed me on the bed, kissing my lips and admiring my body before sucking on my breasts. He looked at me for a moment, his hand stroking his own erection while I nodded in agreement, silently asking him to take me with his eleven-inch member. It was as if he wanted me to guide him, feeling guilty for wanting to sleep with his best friend's girlfriend. But I didn't care about guilt in that moment. All I knew is that I was incredibly aroused and ready for him to fill me up.

"This isn't the time for you to feel guilty, Mark," I thought to myself, "I'm so horny and I need you to fuck me right now." And without hesitation, that's exactly what he did.

Slowly sliding inside of me, I felt a surge of pleasure wash over me as my back arched and his thick shaft filled me up completely. It was like coming back to life after dying; an indescribable feeling that left me moaning uncontrollably.

"OH MY GOD!" I screamed, "OH WOW! OH SHIT! OHHH MY GOODNESS!"

He picked up the pace and started thrusting harder, his wet cock slapping against my pussy with each movement. My juices dripped down onto the floor as he pounded into me relentlessly.

"You like that, baby?" he asked.

"Yes, yes, yes," I responded repeatedly.

Keith was so deep inside Davina's pussy that he didn't even notice when Mark carried me into another room. Finally alone, he placed me on the bed and kissed my lips again. "I've wanted you for so long, baby," he whispered in my ear. Now let me make this clear: I don't know if it was the drugs or alcohol running through my system, but those words definitely came out of his mouth because in that moment he made love to me. He expressed his feelings for me, and I couldn't believe it. But it felt so good, like no one had ever made me feel before. And I couldn't deny that I felt the same way. The moment was overwhelming, and I couldn't resist it. As shocking as his confession was, I couldn't say that I didn't feel the same way.

I could feel his hot breath on my neck as he whispered in my ear.

"Who do you think I was recording, darling? Do you think I give a damn about those two idiots out there?"

His tone was possessive, and it sent shivers down my spine. He continued.

"Your body is incredible. That's why everyone wants a piece of you. Can I have all of you, baby?"

My heart raced as I eagerly replied.

"Yes, of course."

In that moment, he became wild and aggressive with me. He opened my legs and used his tongue to ravish my vagina, sending waves of pleasure through every inch of my body.

"You taste amazing," he moaned before kissing me deeply.

The taste of our combined fluids lingered on his lips, igniting a fire within me. What was happening? Was I falling in love with my boyfriend's friend? He had always looked at me sweetly before, but never like this. It was usually more of a protective look, like a brother or sister. But now it was different.

"I want you to myself," he begged as he flipped me over and entered my ass without warning.

My mind was in a haze from the alcohol and drugs, but the intensity of his thrusts brought me back to reality.

"No, wait, please, oh my goodness," I begged as he continued to pound into me with relentless force.

"Do you like this, baby? Tell me if you want me to stop," he asked between grunts as we both sweated under his dominant movements.

"No, don't stop," I cried out in ecstasy as he reached his peak inside me.

"That's it, let go," I assured him as he collapsed onto me and held me tightly against his chest.

Minutes later, he pulled out and licked all the cum from my backside before sucking on every last drop. Then, his skilled tongue made its way back up to my clit and he expertly brought me to three more orgasms before swallowing every drop. He then kissed his way down my stomach before moving back up to my nipples and lips, showering me with affection once again. After admiring my body in awe, he reluctantly left the room, leaving me wondering what else he could possibly have in store for me. My thoughts raced as I tried to process everything that had just happened. He had already pleasured me in every way imaginable, and now he was saying there was more? I was completely drained and weak from the alcohol and drugs, not to mention ten intense orgasms in one hour. I barely remember what happened after he left, but I do recall passing out from exhaustion.

It had been two years since that unforgettable night, and we all had a great time. Some of us may have enjoyed it more than others. As I entered my living room, my phone started ringing with a familiar tune. With a sigh, I answered the call and heard the voice of my boyfriend, Keith, on the other end. He sounded exhausted from work, promising to call me back later.

I replied with an "I love you" before hanging up and making my way to the bedroom.

But as I pushed open the door, my heart skipped a beat at the sight that greeted me. There he was - Mark, the man with an eleven-inch penis that I couldn't resist. He lay on the bed, his body completely exposed and ready for me. The soft light filtering through the window highlighted every curve and muscle of his sculpted body, making him look like a Greek god in human form. My breath caught in my throat as I took in the sight - his broad shoulders, defined abs, and strong thighs.

Despite knowing that this secret affair couldn't last forever, I couldn't help but feel a sense of exhilaration at seeing Mark lying there before me. A small smile tugged at my lips as I gazed at him admiringly. But as much as I wanted our relationship to be out in the open, I knew it would only bring chaos and pain to everyone involved. Keith would eventually find out about us, and I was getting tired of hiding our passionate encounters. But in that moment, all thoughts of Keith disappeared as Mark's intense gaze locked onto mine. There shouldn't be anything secretive about this man who brought me so much pleasure and fulfillment - the man with a unique endowment that drove me wild with desire every time we were together. For he, and his eleven-inch penis was my fetish.

Penitentiary Sex

No, I didn't plan to be his jailhouse whore,
Thrown in a cell, treated like dirt on the floor,
But amidst the darkness, a glimmer of light,
His presence ignited a fire, burning.

~

His manhood, an impressive ten-inch in size,
Captivated me completely, took me by surprise,
I was spellbound, enchanted; I couldn't resist,
Drawn to him like a moth to a flame, I persist.

~

So don't judge or mock my unconventional choice,
Love knows no boundaries, it has its own voice,
In the depths of despair, we found our salvation,
A connection formed beyond society's dictation.

Nine

Harry

Listen, I was a rebellious young man, always pushing the boundaries and engaging in activities that would shock most people. I delved into a world of darkness and desire that few dare to explore. I reveled in the thrill of engaging in acts that satisfied my deepest cravings. But there was one encounter that took me to an entirely different level. It happened in 2009 when I was just twenty-five years old, a time when I was no stranger to brushes with the law. Society's rules meant nothing to me; I stole, fought, and indulged in sexual encounters without remorse. My mother had long lost control over me, so it baffled me why the police thought they could rein me in.

The last time I found myself behind bars, locked away in a cold, dreary cell, I couldn't help but ponder my innocence. It seemed that no matter what I did, the authorities always found a way to pin the blame on me. Perhaps it was because of my striking good looks, or maybe they simply enjoyed the thrill of playing with my life like a twisted game. As I paced back and forth in that dimly lit prison cell for what felt like an eternity, a deep weariness settled within me. The constant cycle of getting arrested and thrown back into this hellhole was draining my soul. But amidst the exhaustion, there was another craving that gnawed at me relentlessly - a primal desire that only grew stronger with each passing day. In this confined space devoid of any female presence, my lust burned hotter than ever before. The absence of willing companionship left me longing for release, driving my mind to wander into realms of dirty fantasies and role play scenarios. Imprisonment had become not only a punishment for crimes I didn't commit but also an opportunity to explore the depths of my insatiable impulse.

As I was led to my assigned cell, I couldn't help but notice the presence of the alluring female prison guards. They were always teasing, strutting around in their form-fitting police uniforms, flaunting their curves without a care in the world. It was clear they enjoyed the power they held over the inmates, but I saw through their facade. They may have thought they were sly, but I knew exactly what game they were playing. However, getting one of those women guards wasn't as simple as having a charming personality or being a smooth talker. No, it took a certain kind of man to capture their attention - someone with an undeniable air of dominance and confidence. Only a well-endowed, fearless individual could hope to catch their eye.

As I made my way through the corridors, three hulking figures locked eyes with me. They clearly recognized me as fresh meat, ready to be dominated and broken down. But little did they know that I had spent enough time in this unforgiving environment to recognize intimidation when it stared me in the face. Tonight was not the night for them to assert their dominance over me; I would not allow it. With a steely resolve and an unwavering sense of self-assuredness, I entered my cell knowing that I would not be easily swayed or controlled by anyone within these prison walls. My experience had taught me how to navigate these treacherous waters, and tonight, I would prove that no one could break my spirit or diminish my strength.

The guard begrudgingly handed me my belongings, his expression revealing his annoyance at my request. With a curt nod, he motioned for me to follow him towards my assigned bunk. As we walked, I couldn't help but feel a sense of dread knowing that I would be stuck on the top bunk once again. The top bunk had always been a source of frustration for me – cramped, uncomfortable, and lacking any sense of privacy. It seemed like fate had a cruel sense of humor. Suppressing my disappointment, I mustered up the courage to speak up.

"Excuse me," I called out to the guard, trying to maintain a polite tone despite my growing frustration. "Is there any way I could possibly get a bottom bunk? It would really make a difference for me."

The guard glanced at me with an incredulous look before responding in a dismissive tone.

"Are you kidding? We're full up here. You'll have to make do with what you've got," he retorted, sounding entirely unsympathetic to my predicament.

Resigned to my fate, I trudged up the narrow staircase leading to the top bunk. Each step felt heavier than the last as I reluctantly ascended to my less-than-ideal sleeping arrangement. As I settled into the uncomfortable mattress, surrounded by unfamiliar faces and the sounds of restless sleepers, I couldn't help but curse my luck silently. Sleeping on the top bunk was not just an inconvenience; it was a constant reminder of how circumstances can conspire against you. But amidst all the discomfort and frustration, there was a flicker of determination within me – a resolve to endure and rise above whatever challenges lay ahead in this unfamiliar environment. The three men said nothing, just continued playing their card games as I moaned like a little bitch to myself. The guard then left our cell, closing the door behind him. Seconds later, the Latin guy stood up and walked over to my bed, his towering presence casting a shadow over me. At six foot five inches, he commanded attention without even trying. He had an air of authority that intrigued me, a dangerous allure that made my heart race.

"Hey, what's your name?" he asked, his deep voice resonating in the small space.

"I'm Harry," I replied, feeling a mix of nervousness and curiosity.

Without answering my question directly, he leaned in closer and whispered in my ear.

"In this prison, we have our own set of rules. You'll learn to respect your cell mates and keep your mouth shut."

His words sent shivers down my spine as I realized the power dynamics at play. It was clear that obedience was not optional in this confined world of secrets and desires. As I looked into his intense gaze, I sensed a hint of dominance that ignited something deep within me. From that moment on, I knew there was no turning back. I would embrace the darkness and delve into the forbidden world of role play and fetishism that existed behind these prison walls. It was a journey that would push boundaries and challenge everything I thought I knew about myself. Little did I know then just how far down the rabbit hole I was about to go. I nodded my head, trying not to show how scared I was.

'Well damn,' I thought to myself, 'they're about to fuck me up.'

Those first few days behind bars were surprisingly uneventful - no fights, no arguments, and no trouble. It gave me a false sense of security, thinking that this prison life might be easier than anticipated. But oh boy, was I wrong.

A couple of days later, as I stood in front of the sink brushing my teeth, I could feel the tension in the air. The atmosphere was thick, like something was about to go down. And sure enough, as I turned around to climb onto my bunk, Travis appeared before me. His presence alone sent shivers down my spine. Travis, with his towering stature and bulging muscles, looked like he could crush me with a single blow. His grip on my wrist was tight and unyielding, making it clear that resistance was futile. In that moment, all I could do was try to maintain a facade of strength while fear coursed through my veins.

As he held onto me, Travis leaned in close and whispered into my ear with a voice that sent chills down my spine. He spoke in hushed tones about his desires and fetishes, revealing a side of him that I never expected to encounter in this prison environment. It became evident that for some inmates, this place served as more than just a punishment - it became an outlet for their darkest fantasies. With each passing second under Travis's powerful grasp, the reality of what prison truly entailed started to sink in. No longer could I ignore the undercurrents of desire and fetishism that ran through these walls. It became clear that survival behind bars meant navigating not only physical violence but also the twisted dynamics of power and pleasure. In that moment, I realized that my journey through this prison would be far from ordinary. It would be a twisted dance of dominance and submission, where every move I made would have consequences. And as Travis released his grip on my wrist, I knew that this was just the beginning of a dangerous game that I had unwillingly become a part of.

"You're sleeping with me tonight," he boldly declared. I nonchalantly shrugged, not wanting to appear too eager or resistant.

"WHAT! Listen, I'm not trying to be rude or anything, but sir, um, no thanks," I calmly responded.

He chuckled softly, his laughter tainted by the stains of his cigarettes on his teeth. Surprisingly, there was a certain charm to him when he smiled. It made me wonder why someone like him would be incarcerated; perhaps it was for murder, maybe even multiple killings and arson committed with his bare hands. Trust me, he looked like a formidable force. I didn't want to become another victim of his strength that night; I had mentally prepared myself for the harsh realities of prison.

As the tension hung in the air, he leaned closer and whispered into my ear.

"You misunderstand me. I meant that we're going to play a little game tonight."

Intrigued yet cautious, I asked him what kind of game he had in mind. There was a mischievous glint in his eyes as he revealed his plan - a daring role-playing scenario inspired by our darkest fantasies. The thought of indulging in such forbidden desires within the confines of this prison cell both excited and terrified me. With a newfound sense of anticipation and danger coursing through my veins, I hesitantly agreed to partake in this illicit escapade. Little did I know that this encounter would push the boundaries of pleasure and reality in ways I had never imagined before. I knew exactly what had transpired, and I was fully aware of the situation at hand. Mr. Hulk, with his imposing presence, was about to engage in some intense activities with me, if you catch my drift. However, I wasn't mentally prepared for the level of intensity he was about to bring.

In that moment, it dawned on me that there were only two possible outcomes: either I would meet my demise or my posterior would suffer greatly. So, on that fateful night, I made the decision to prioritize the well-being of my backside.

"Is your ass properly cleansed?" he asked with a sternness in his voice.

"Well, umm... yeah, I suppose so," I stammered in response.

"Make your way to the sink and thoroughly cleanse that ass," he commanded as he casually lit a cigarette.

As I obediently followed his instructions and cleaned myself up, a mix of anticipation and apprehension filled the air. Little did I know what lay ahead in this unconventional encounter. I made my way across the cramped cell towards the solitary sink, feeling the cold metal against my skin as I removed my pants. With a sense of liberation, I used my hands to cleanse myself, ensuring every inch was thoroughly washed. Despite the harsh conditions, I took pride in maintaining cleanliness even in this confined space. As I focused on the task at hand, I noticed Mr. Hulk's gaze fixated on me. His eyes were filled with desire and anticipation, his own arousal evident in his growing excitement. The thought crossed my mind that perhaps this unexpected attraction could work to my advantage within these prison walls. An intriguing idea formed in my mind as I considered the possibilities.

"The wetter he becomes," I pondered silently, "the smoother our connection will be."

It was a notion that both excited and intrigued me; an opportunity to explore uncharted territory within the realm of pleasure. In this unconventional environment, where desires often remained suppressed, it was exhilarating to consider indulging in forbidden fantasies. The potential for role play and fetishism hung heavy in the air, igniting a fire within me that refused to be extinguished. As I completed my cleansing ritual, a newfound confidence welled up inside me. The power dynamics within this cell seemed to shift ever so slightly with each passing moment. A game of seduction began to unfold, fueled by unspoken desires and hidden passions. In this confined space, where freedom was scarce and boundaries blurred, we embraced the opportunity to explore our innermost cravings without judgment or reservation. A dance of dominance and submission awaited us—a tantalizing journey that would leave an indelible mark on our souls.

I finished off my shower, the water cascading down my body as I rinsed away the dirt and grime. Grabbing my trousers, I used them to wipe off the remaining droplets from my skin. With a sense of purpose, I walked over to him, my cellmate, who lay on his bed. It was the one directly below mine, offering a different level of comfort. But as I climbed in beside him, a strong scent of sweat and sex permeated the air.

It was evident that he had been here for quite some time, immersed in this world of confinement and desire. Lying next to him, I could feel his presence enveloping me. He extinguished his cigarette, creating an ambiance filled with keenness. As I buried my face into the sheets, the musky odor intensified, heightening my senses. He positioned me on all fours, using prison jargon to describe our arrangement. His hands were robust and skilled, like those of a machinist. They firmly grasped my buttocks, exerting a calculated pressure that sent waves of pleasure through me. With a single palm, he reached beneath me and took hold of my flaccid cock and balls. The sensation was both intense and exhilarating; his grasp enveloped me completely. In that moment, our connection transcended the confines of our prison walls, embracing the rawness and vulnerability that exists within us all.

"Your skin feels like a baby's bottom," he whispered in my ear.

The unexpected compliment caught me off guard, leaving me speechless and unsure of how to respond. His touch was gentle yet firm as he explored the contours of my body, his hands gliding smoothly over my skin. In that moment, I realized the power of suspense and the allure of the unknown. It was as if we were both participants in a forbidden dance, embracing our darkest desires without judgment or inhibition.

With each touch, a new layer of sensation unfolded, heightening our connection and deepening our shared pleasure. Our bodies
became instruments of pleasure, orchestrating a symphony of desire
that echoed through the air. His touch ignited a fire within me,
awakening desires I never knew existed. As he continued to explore
every inch of my being, I surrendered myself completely to the
moment. In this world we had created together, there were no rules
or limitations; only raw passion and unbridled ecstasy. My cries of
agony were muffled by the plush pillows, my teeth clenched tight as
I shut my eyes against the pain.

"Do you enjoy this, my love?" he taunted, his voice dripping
with smugness.

Despite the initial discomfort, I found myself beginning to relish
the sensation of his strapping body pressed against mine.

"Oh yes, it's divine," I moaned, my words lost in the soft fabric
of the pillows.

"You truly are a force to be reckoned with, Mr Hulk." His laughter echoed through the room at my playful nickname for him.

"Is that what you wish to call me now?" he asked, increasing the
intensity of his thrusts.

"Yes, my formidable and insatiable Mr Motherfucking Hulk," I
gasped, fighting for breath between each word.

"We're bound together now, husband and wife. Do you comprehend that?" He says as he kept repeating his love for me.

The unrelenting rhythm of our lovemaking continued, a mix of torment and ecstasy that I was willing to endure for the man who had come to love.

The thrusting continued relentlessly, each movement a mix of pleasure and pain that took me into another world. He smacked my ass, causing it to wiggle, then pulling on my shoulder length hair he bent my neck, kissing me passionately as he continued to pleasure me. The intensity of his touch sent shivers down my spine, igniting a fire within me that I couldn't resist. My body arched in response to his expert movements, craving more of his intoxicating touch. Every thrust was a delicious torment, driving me closer to the edge of ecstasy. As the pleasure built inside me, I could feel myself losing control, surrendering completely to the primal desires that consumed us both. Sweat glistened on our bodies as we moved together in perfect harmony, lost in a world of forbidden pleasure. With each moan and gasp that escaped our lips, we pushed the boundaries of pleasure further and further. The room filled with an electric energy as our bodies collided in a symphony of lust and desire. In that moment, nothing else mattered except the raw passion between us.

We were prisoners to our own carnal desires, embracing every dark fantasy and fetish without shame or judgment. I could feel the warm, pulsating sensation as his penis released its load deep inside me, filling me with a mixture of pleasure and satisfaction. As he withdrew from my trembling body, a rush of cool air brushed against my skin, causing goosebumps to form in its wake. It was a moment of vulnerability and intimacy that heightened the intensity of our connection.

With his penis no longer inside me, he shifted his attention to another erogenous zone - my ass. His tongue delved into the depths of my most intimate area, exploring and pleasuring me in ways I had never experienced before. The combination of his oral skills and the lingering taste of his own essence sent waves of pleasure coursing through my body. In that position, with my head pulled back by his strong grip, our lips met in a passionate kiss. It was a deliciously dirty exchange as he shared the remnants of his release with me. I willingly accepted his gift, savoring the salty sweetness on my tongue before obediently swallowing every drop. As he released my head from his grasp, he returned to lavishing attention on my ass, teasing and tantalizing me with each sensual lick. It was an incredible sight to behold - a man who knew exactly how to worship and fulfill me.

In that surreal moment, I couldn't help but be overwhelmed by the sheer magic unfolding before me. It was as if we had entered into our own private world where inhibitions were shed and passions ran wild. The intensity of our connection transcended mere physical pleasure; it was a journey into the realm of fantasy and fulfillment. Every touch, every kiss, every whispered word sent shivers down my spine and ignited a fire within me that burned hotter than ever before. It was a testament to the power of exploration and embracing one's sexuality without shame or judgment. As he skillfully explored the contours of my backside with his tongue, his expert mouth moved to my testicles, enveloping them in a wet, sensual embrace. With my throbbing manhood now nestled between his lips, I could feel the warmth and intensity building within me. His oral prowess intensified, coaxing me closer to the edge of ecstasy.

Lost in the whirlwind of pleasure, a tantalizing question crossed my mind: Who was truly in control in this passionate exchange?

Was it him, with his insatiable hunger for every inch of me? Or was it me, surrendering myself to the intoxicating power of his desire? He displayed an unprecedented level of devotion as he indulged in the most intimate parts of my body. The way he eagerly consumed every drop of my essence made me wonder if there was a hint of domination lurking beneath his seemingly submissive demeanour. I chuckled to myself as my imagination took off, envisioning all the thrilling possibilities that lay ahead. With a firm grip, I pressed his head down onto my throbbing shaft, revelling in the power exchange of dominance and submission. Guiding him with a commanding voice, I urged him to intensify his oral skills, knowing that his passion matched mine perfectly. In that moment, it became clear to me that our connection was more than just physical; it was a deep and everlasting bond.

After experiencing mind-blowing pleasure multiple times, he gently guided me to turn around, positioning me so that my back was against his chest. His strong arms enveloped me protectively, creating an intoxicating sense of safety. With tenderness and purpose, he entered me one final time that night, his rhythmic thrusts lulling us both into a blissful state of exhaustion. As we lay intertwined in the aftermath of our passionate encounter, I couldn't help but reflect on the profound connection we shared. Our exploration of pleasure knew no bounds. The allure of role play and fetishism had brought us together in ways we never thought possible.

In the dimly lit room, our bodies tangled in a delicious embrace, I reveled in the thought of our next encounter. The idea of exploring new realms of pleasure excited me beyond measure; there were no limits to what we could experience together. The tantalizing prospect of indulging in passions like prison sex and other forbidden fantasies only fueled our insatiable appetite for each other. His snores grew in volume, filling the room with a symphony of slumber. As I lay nestled in his arms, my eyelids heavy with exhaustion, I too succumbed to the embrace of sleep. The gentle rhythm of our breaths intertwined, creating a harmony that echoed through the stillness of the night. As the intimacy between us waned, I could feel a bittersweet ache in my heart. Our connection, forged in the heat of passion and desire, now fading like embers slowly losing their glow. Yet, there was an undeniable allure to this forbidden love affair, a taste of danger that thrilled and terrified me in equal measure.

In the darkness, my thoughts drifted to the other men who shared our confinement. Their presence lingered like a shadow on the edge of my consciousness. I wondered if they too reveled in their secret desires and clandestine encounters. Perhaps behind closed doors, they explored fantasies that mirrored our own. In this world where rules were bent and boundaries blurred, silence was our currency. No one dared speak of what transpired under the cover of night; it was an unspoken pact among inmates. Each man locked away his secrets and guarded them fiercely, knowing that discovery would bring consequences far more severe than any punishment behind bars.

Weeks later, as you can guess, I found myself completely enthralled by him. He had become the center of my universe, and I willingly embraced the role he assigned me. I became his devoted submissive, eager to fulfill his every need. The boundaries of our relationship blurred as I willingly surrendered control. In addition to taking care of our basic needs, I began exploring new realms of pleasure with him. Our encounters were filled with intense passion and an unquenchable hunger for each other's bodies. The risk of getting caught only heightened the excitement we felt. There were moments when our desires led us astray, resulting in disciplinary actions that took me away from him. But even in those solitary confinements, my thoughts revolved around him and the insatiable craving for his touch. It was a sacrifice I was willing to make for the ecstasy he brought into my life. His commanding presence and his sizable manhood consumed my thoughts, constantly reminding me of the depths of my devotion to him.

Four years later, I finally walked out of those prison gates, a free man once again. It was a bittersweet feeling, knowing that I had fulfilled my promise to stay in touch with him until his release. I had dedicated so much of my time and effort to taking care of him, even sending him money when he needed it most. But little did I know, behind those cold prison walls, he was indulging in the forbidden pleasures with another man. The discovery shattered me. How could he do this to me after all I had done for him? The betrayal cut deep, leaving scars that would take time to heal. Yet, as I reflect on my life I realize that things have changed. While my sexual preferences and desires remain unchanged, I no longer seek validation or satisfaction through the dangerous allure of prison life.

I've grown wiser and more discerning in my choices. My appetite for pleasure is still insatiable, but I've learned to explore new realms of sexuality beyond the confines of prison walls. Role play has become an exciting part of my intimate encounters, allowing me to fulfill hidden fantasies and indulge in passion without the risks associated with incarceration. As for prison sex and fetishism, they are experiences from a bygone era. They served their purpose at a time when I craved connection and intimacy amidst the desolation of confinement. Now, I embrace a world where men are free to explore their desires openly and consensually.

So yes, while certain elements of my past still linger within me, reminding me of where I've been and who I once was, they no longer define me completely. Instead, they serve as reminders of the journey I've undertaken towards self-discovery and liberation. With each passing day, I continue to grow stronger and more confident in my own skin. And as for him - the one who betrayed my trust - I have forgiven him, not for his sake, but for my own peace of mind. The shackles of resentment and anger no longer bind me.

I've moved on, ready to embrace a future that is filled with love, pleasure, and freedom. I've managed to avoid any major mishaps, and I am now blissfully engaged to a stunningly handsome Russian man who dotes on me endlessly. Of course, life has its ups and downs, but losing that alluring gentleman was undeniably a significant blow for me. He was the kind of catch that turned heads and caused hearts to flutter with just one glance.

Libertine

I must confess, I started as a novice in this game,
But I left with victory, my triumph is not in vain.
Explored new realms of pleasure, no limits to constrain,
Indulged in desires, unashamed of being profane.
~

They were a couple unlike any other, I must proclaim,
Together we danced, an erotic tango with no shame.
He dove deep inside me, like a diver chasing fame,
Leaving me breathless, as if he was playing a game.
~

I entered that room carrying some extra weight,
But the passion we shared made my body deflate.
Each thrust and moan propelled my transformation's rate,
Leaving me leaner, lighter, feeling truly great.
~

Her breasts were a masterpiece, soft lips a tempting lure,
Our tongues intertwined, a dance that would endure.
She pleasured his manhood with such skill and allure,
I tasted the ecstasy deep within my core.
~

In this forbidden tryst, we embraced our inner sinner,
From dusk till dawn, our bodies entwined like a rhapsody
spinner.
~
We indulged in pleasures that made us all shimmer,
Oh what a night it was, an unforgettable winner.

Ten

Dave

I am not afraid to admit that I was a beginner when it came to exploring my sexual desires. I went in feeling like a loser, unsure of what to expect or how I would handle it. But little did I know, this experience would transform me into a winner, both sexually and personally. As I delved into the world of swingers and fetishes, I realized that there were endless possibilities for pleasure and connection. It was liberating to be surrounded by individuals who shared my curiosity and openness. Together, we pushed the boundaries of pleasure, exploring new positions, techniques, and fantasies. One thing that struck me was the diversity within this community. People from all walks of life came together in pursuit of their desires. It was fascinating to witness how different fetishes and preferences could coexist harmoniously, without judgment or shame.

Each encounter became an opportunity for growth and self-discovery. The intimate connections I formed with others allowed me to explore aspects of myself that I had previously ignored or denied. It was as if my own sexuality had been waiting patiently for this moment to fully blossom. In these encounters, there was no room for inhibitions or holding back. It was a space where passion flowed freely and boundaries were discussed and respected. From sensual massages to intense role-playing sessions, every experience added a new layer of excitement and satisfaction.

But amidst all the novelty and exploration, one thing remained constant - the power of consent. It was refreshing to be part of a community that held consent in such high regard. Every interaction began with clear communication and mutual agreement, ensuring that everyone involved felt safe and comfortable throughout. Ever since the age of thirty, my fantasies and desires were starting to develop, day after day. I could feel my desires expanding; my thoughts beginning to come to fruition, almost as if it was taking over my life. But I wouldn't allow it, I had to keep these feelings under control, but I couldn't resist their allure. The more I tried to suppress them, the stronger they became, like a wildfire burning within me. It was as if my entire being craved for the forbidden pleasures that lay beyond societal norms.

I found solace in exploring the world of swingers and fetishes, diving deep into an underground realm where inhibitions were shed like old skins. The allure of experiencing new sexual encounters with like-minded individuals consumed me. The anticipation of discovering uncharted territories of pleasure made my heart race with excitement. Within this liberated community, pussy eating and dick sucking were celebrated as art forms. People enjoyed the joy of giving and receiving pleasure without judgment or shame. It was an intoxicating dance of seduction and satisfaction that transcended the boundaries of conventional relationships. The thrill of indulging in these carnal adventures ignited a fire within me that burned brighter than ever before. It was a journey of self-discovery and liberation, where every encounter pushed me further towards embracing my true desires.

Ever since that pivotal age of thirty, I embarked on a journey that would forever change me. I embraced my fantasies and desires, allowing them to shape me into a person unafraid of pushing boundaries and exploring the depths of pleasure. It was a transformative experience that taught me the power of embracing one's true self, even if it meant venturing into uncharted territories of sexual exploration. Back then, I had just arrived in the United Kingdom for work. I had moved over from Spain, ready to embark on a new chapter in my life. As an adventurous soul, I was eager to explore not only the city but also my own desires. Being in a foreign country allowed me the freedom to delve into uncharted territories of pleasure. The online world became my sanctuary, a place where I could indulge in sexual fantasies and explore the depths of my desires. It was exhilarating to connect with like-minded individuals who shared my insatiable appetite for sex. Through virtual encounters, I discovered a world of swingers, fetishes, and taboo pleasures that ignited a fire within me.

At this point, a part of me grew weary of existing in the confines of this imagined realm. I yearned to embrace and explore the myriad desires that danced within my mind. It was during this quest for liberation that I stumbled upon a virtual oasis known as Fab-swingers, a website that beckoned me with its promises of unbridled pleasures. As I delved deeper into the sea of enticing profiles and tantalizing photographs, my eyes were opened to an expansive universe of eroticism, where boundaries dissolved and inhibitions crumbled. It became evident that this world was not confined to mere carnal indulgence; it encompassed an entire spectrum of passions, fetishes, and unconventional predilections. And so, with a mixture of trepidation and anticipation coursing through my veins, I dared to embark on a journey that would challenge societal norms and redefine the limits of pleasure. In this realm, pussy eating became an art form, dick sucking an act of worship, and fucking an expression of raw desire.

As I continued to navigate through the profiles, I stumbled upon a captivating couple who caught my attention. This husband and wife duo seemed incredibly open-minded and adventurous in their desires. Their profile exuded a sense of confidence and clarity, leaving no room for ambiguity. They were seeking more than just the conventional.

"lay there and let me fuck you kind of things."

Their interests delved into the realms of bondage, whips, and a variety of other tantalizing fetishes that piqued my curiosity. Instead of being repulsed by their explicit preferences, I found myself becoming even more intrigued. The thought of exploring these uncharted territories excited me beyond measure. I craved the opportunity to immerse myself in this new realm of pleasure and indulge in experiences that were far from ordinary. The couple's openness about their desires only powered my eagerness to delve deeper into this world of sexual exploration. It was refreshing to encounter individuals who knew exactly what they wanted and weren't afraid to express it. Their detailed profile showcased their understanding of their own needs and made it clear that they were looking for nothing less than mind-blowing encounters. Their authenticity was undeniable, and it instantly established a level of trust between us. It was evident that they had ventured down this path before, which only heightened my excitement further. The prospect of engaging with them promised an unforgettable adventure filled with passion, pleasure, and intensity.

Intrigued by the possibilities that lay ahead, I couldn't help but anticipate the electrifying moments we would share together. The allure of embracing bondage, experimenting with whips, and exploring some deliciously naughty disguises enticed me like never before. This encounter had all the makings of an extraordinary experience - one that would push boundaries, challenge inhibitions, and leave us all craving for more. With each swipe through their profile pictures and every word read from their enticing description, my eagerness grew exponentially. The wait to satisfy these desires felt excruciating, but I knew that the wait would only intensify the pleasure that awaited us. They wanted a nice, handsome young man with a big cock, and I can assure you that I fit that description perfectly. Intrigued by their desires, I mustered up the courage to engage in conversation with them. Admittedly, I was quite nervous at first, as this was uncharted territory for me. How does one even begin to navigate such unconventional discussions? Maybe I could say something like:

"Do forgive my forwardness, "but your profile piqued my interest. My name is Dave, and I find myself drawn to exploring the pleasures of your wife while you indulge in the exquisite art of pleasuring my ample balls." Okay, maybe not, maybe I should be a little more calm, I thought to myself.

It dawned on me that there was no universally accepted approach to these types of conversations. Each encounter would require its own unique finesse. So, drawing from the wisdom imparted by my dear mother, I decided to take a more nuanced route.

"Greetings," I began with a hint of playfulness, "I couldn't help but be captivated by your profile. Allow me to introduce myself as Dave, an individual eager to embark on an exhilarating journey of shared desires and tantalizing experiences."

With each exchange, my confidence grew as I navigated the intricate dance of desire and pleasure. It became clear that communication was key in exploring our mutual fantasies and discovering new depths of satisfaction together. So, armed with charm and curiosity, I continued engaging with these intriguing individuals who sought liberation from societal norms and embraced their own unique expressions of passion and pleasure. And so it began – an exhilarating journey of self-discovery and shared pleasure, where the only limit was the depths of our imagination.

'If you didn't have anything nice to say then don't say anything at all', and boy did I have a few nasty things to say about his wife's breasts.

But, I reminded myself of the golden rule and decided to keep those thoughts to myself. Instead, I focused on doing some research and trying to establish a connection with my desires and the provocative picture they had posted. With a surge of confidence, I took the initiative and messaged them. Surprisingly, they turned out to be quite pleasant and approachable individuals. They never had anything negative to say; in fact, they seemed experienced in this realm and knew exactly what words to use to captivate my attention. We eventually progressed from messages to phone calls, where I had the opportunity to speak with both of them. The conversation flowed effortlessly, putting me at ease as I contemplated my decision further.

After sending photos back and forth of all our body parts, a few weeks later they extended an invitation for me to join them at a hotel. Naturally, I eagerly accepted the offer, although my nerves were in overdrive. In the days leading up to our encounter, I experienced a rollercoaster of emotions, oscillating between sheer excitement and a nagging sense of anxiety. The anticipation grew stronger with each passing day, as I yearned for the pleasure of having someone devour my balls. However, a small voice in the back of my mind questioned if I was making the right decision. What if this experience turned out to be more than I could handle? What if they despised the sight of my manhood? These doubts swirled within me, intensifying my nervousness even further.

What if I wasn't good enough for them? I mean, we're talking about two very experienced swingers; they've probably had countless encounters with both men and women. It made me wonder what made me so special in their eyes. The thought that kept lingering in my mind was the fear of the unknown. What if they had some dark, twisted fantasies that involved inflicting pain or humiliation? What if they wanted to explore fetishes that I wasn't comfortable with? The possibilities seemed endless and it sent shivers down my spine. My imagination ran wild with disturbing scenarios. What if they planned to mutilate my body, removing body parts as some sadistic ritual? Or perhaps they desired to dominate me completely, turning me into their submissive plaything. These thoughts haunted me as I prepared to meet them. Deep down, a part of me was excited by the thrill of the unknown. The prospect of exploring new boundaries and discovering hidden desires enticed me. But at the same time, I couldn't help but feel a sense of trepidation.

'Oh dear God, I was going to die.'

My heart started racing as I thought about being killed. I mean, let's face it, the world can be a dangerous place. Especially when you find yourself venturing into uncharted territories like the realm of fetishes and swingers. It's a thrilling and exhilarating experience, but it also comes with its fair share of risks. As I prepared to embark on this journey alone, my mind couldn't help but conjure up all sorts of scenarios. What if things went wrong? What if I found myself in a compromising situation? The unknown was both terrifying and tantalizing. However, instead of succumbing to fear, I chose to embrace the excitement and possibility that awaited me. With each beat of my racing heart, I felt a surge of adrenaline coursing through my veins. This was an adventure unlike any other, one that would push the boundaries of my desires and redefine what it meant to truly live life to the fullest.

On the night of the highly anticipated rendezvous, they provided explicit instructions for me to meet them at a discreet hotel. With a potent mixture of excitement and nervousness, my heart raced within my chest as if it yearned to break free from its confines. Eager to steady my nerves, I promptly arrived at the designated location and sought solace in the embrace of the hotel's bar. Mindful not to intoxicate myself excessively and risk embarrassing missteps, I opted for a moderate consumption of gin, just enough to sedate the relentless palpitations that threatened to betray my composure. I took a deep breath, gathering my nerves as I sat in the hotel bar. Moments later, my phone buzzed, and I saw Diana's name on the screen. She was outside, waiting to pick me up and take me to their home. It was a thrilling feeling that made my heart race. As I finished my drink, I couldn't help but feel a tingling sensation in my groin, a clear sign that he was ready for pleasure. With determination in my eyes, I stood up from the bar stool and confidently walked out of the hotel, ready to explore new boundaries with this adventurous couple.

As I pulled up outside, my eyes were immediately drawn to a stunning woman standing by her car. She exuded an irresistible allure that was even more captivating than her pictures. Her radiant smile beckoned me closer, and I couldn't resist the magnetic pull. With her flowing blonde hair cascading down her back and her sun-kissed skin accentuating her toned physique, she was like a goddess before me. The warmth in her eyes and the excitement in her voice as she waved me over made my heart race with happiness. Closing the distance between us, we embraced like long-lost lovers, exchanging tender kisses on each cheek as if we were celebrating our own private affair. The sight of her blue Mazda convertible, its top down revealing the open sky above, only heightened the intoxicating atmosphere surrounding us. I arrived at their home, where her husband warmly welcomed me. With a glass of white wine in his hands and a wide grin on his face, he exuded an air of excitement. Moments later, his wife appeared, radiating beauty and confidence. As she approached him, she affectionately whispered.

"Hello darling," planting a passionate kiss on his lips.

The sight of their intimacy sparked a tantalizing curiosity within me. A thought crossed my mind: despite the impending adventure that awaited them, he seemed blissfully content. Then again, I doubt they would be able to go through with this kind of stuff if there wasn't any trust between them. That's why I believe they engage in these experiences as a couple. Unsure of how to greet him, I contemplated between a hug, a handshake, or even a kiss for fuck's sake. In the end, I opted for a traditional handshake, but he surprised me by rejecting it and pulling me into a warm embrace. It was an unexpected yet delightful welcome.

"Please come inside," he invited while graciously taking my coat and hanging it on the coat hanger.

His words were reassuring, creating an atmosphere where I could truly make myself comfortable. As I entered the dimly lit dining room, a surge of anticipation coursed through my blood. This was really about to happen, and I couldn't help but feel a mix of excitement and nervousness. In an attempt to calm my racing heart, I made a beeline for the bar and poured myself a generous glass of wine. The smooth liquid cascaded down my throat, its warmth spreading throughout my body, easing the tension that had settled within me. I glanced around, hoping to spot more bottles of this intoxicating elixir, for I knew that tonight I needed more than just a drink to quench my thirst. As the night unfolded, laughter filled the air as we indulged in witty banter and playful exchanges. Each sip of wine emboldened us further, breaking down barriers and allowing our inhibitions to crumble away.

The atmosphere was charged with an undeniable electricity, as if every passing moment brought us closer to a thrilling climax. Conversations veered into uncharted territory, exploring desires and fantasies that were once hidden in the recesses of our minds. The night continued to unfold, and the alcohol flowed freely, surging our inhibitions. With each passing moment, our conversations grew bolder, laced with innuendos and playful banter. We revelled in the comfort we had established, knowing that this was a night of exploration and pleasure. Although we had already delved into intimate discussions during our previous phone calls, there was an electric anticipation in the air, hinting at surprises yet to come. And then, like a flicker of desire igniting, his wife's gaze shifted towards me with an unmistakable lustful hunger.

Her words dripped with seduction as she coyly wondered aloud about the tantalizing mystery hidden beneath my tracksuit bottoms. Her mischievous smile conveyed her eagerness to uncover every inch of my body, leaving nothing to the imagination. Our eyes locked in a heated exchange, silently communicating our shared desires and unspoken fantasies. It was as if the room itself became charged with an intoxicating energy.

"I wonder what your body looks like underneath those tracksuit bottoms," she said with a big smile on her face.

Her words hung in the air, charged with curiosity. As I gazed into her eyes, a rush of desire surged through me, pushing forward my every move. Without hesitation, I allowed my hands to graze the fabric of my tracksuit bottoms, teasingly tracing the contours of my body. The thought of revealing myself to her sent shivers down my spine. With each passing second, the room grew hotter, the air thick with an electrifying tension. Her husband watched intently from his seat at the dining room table, his eyes fixated on me as if he were witnessing something forbidden delicious. I couldn't help but wonder what fantasies were brewing in his mind, what secret desires lay hidden beneath his composed exterior.

As I slowly peeled off my clothes, piece by tantalizing piece, her widened eyes betrayed a mixture of awe and hunger. It was as if she had never encountered an eight-inch masterpiece before. I revelled in the power that pulsed through me, knowing that I held their undivided attention. In that moment, I couldn't help but ponder the size of her husband's own manhood. Was it larger than mine?

Did he possess a hidden prowess that matched his wife's insatiable appetite? The possibilities danced in my mind, adding an extra layer of excitement to our forbidden encounter. With my body now fully exposed before them, I stood there unashamed and ready to embrace whatever pleasures lay ahead. Little did I know that this intimate rendezvous would be just the beginning of a journey into a world where boundaries blurred and desires were set free.

I was completely consumed by the moment, my thoughts focused solely on the intense pleasure that awaited me. Standing there, my hand wrapped around my throbbing member, I couldn't tear my eyes away from her enticing figure. The feeling was electric as I yearned for the sensation of my erection being enveloped by her warm, inviting mouth. It was as if she had tapped into my deepest desires, knowing exactly what I craved. With a seductive smile, she rose from her seat and beckoned me closer to the couch. Words were unnecessary; her actions spoke volumes as she eagerly took hold of my pulsating shaft and guided it between her lips. The wetness of her mouth sent shivers down my spine, amplifying the pleasure coursing through every fiber of my being. Her skills were unparalleled as she expertly worked her magic, leaving me with nothing but pure ecstasy. For what seemed like an eternity, she lavished attention upon me, her petite mouth valiantly attempting to accommodate every inch of my throbbing cock while simultaneously teasing and caressing my balls with tantalizing precision.

She then ran her tongue over my balls, teasing them, licking them, and playing with them, driving me wild with desire. Minutes later, she surprised me by sliding her tongue inside my ass, exploring that especially sensitive spot and sending waves of pleasure through my body. Her expertise was unmatched as she continued to suck on one big testicle at a time, then both of them simultaneously, intensifying the sensations coursing through me. With each gentle pop of my ball between her lips, I couldn't help but moan uncontrollably as ecstasy took over. As I watched in awe, my cock stood proudly erect, throbbing with anticipation of what was to come next. She wasted no time and began bobbing her mouth up and down on it, competently using her tongue on the upstroke to heighten the pleasure while expertly massaging my balls with her hands.

As she continued to suck on my big dick, her focus intensified, entering a state of heightened awareness solely dedicated to pleasuring me. I held onto her head, guiding her movements with caution, not wanting to overwhelm her. With my head tilted back, pleasure consumed me, causing moans and groans to escape my lips uncontrollably. My attention then shifted towards her husband, who was pouring himself another drink and removing his shoes. The sight of him preparing himself only expanded my desire further.

"Bring yourself closer to me, baby," she whispered seductively, pulling me towards the couch. Her words hung in the air like an invitation that could not be refused.

"Can I take your bra off?" I asked politely.

"Of course, you can," she replied.

With a swift motion, she unhooked the clasp and let the bra fall to the floor. As her breasts were freed, I couldn't resist but to admire their perfect shape and inviting allure. Her desire was evident as she guided me towards her chest, whispering softly.

"Suck on them, please." Eagerly, I took her nipple into my mouth, swirling my tongue around it in sensual circles.

Her moans of pleasure only increased my own arousal. With each passionate kiss exchanged between us, the heat intensified. Feeling the urgency in the air, she swiftly removed her skirt, exposing herself fully to me. We were both aware of her husband's presence nearby, his eyes locked onto our intimate encounter. As if taunting him further, she leaned in even closer and whispered in my ear;

"I want you inside me."

The desire between us became overwhelming; there was no denying that we both craved each other passionately. Without hesitation or question, our bodies collided in a frenzy of lust and desire that left us breathless and fulfilled. I plunged my throbbing member deep into her slick, aroused pussy. The sensation of her moistness enveloping me sent shivers of pleasure coursing through my body. As I began to thrust, she let out a series of intoxicating moans, her desire echoing in the room. Our lips locked in a passionate embrace, her husband's presence only adding to the forbidden excitement that pulsed between us. With each movement, the intensity grew, fuelled by the knowledge that we were exploring our deepest desires without inhibition. In this uninhibited moment of sexual exploration, our bodies intertwined and danced to the rhythm of our insatiable lust.

I continued to thrust with intensity, the pleasure building within me. As I watched him standing there, pleasuring himself, a surge of excitement coursed through my veins. There was something undeniably arousing about this forbidden act unfolding before my eyes. His display of raw emotions only increased my own lust, urging me to push harder and deeper into her. The way she screamed out in both agony and ecstasy only heightened my enjoyment. I admired at how tight her pussy felt, each tight grip around my member driving me closer to the edge of bliss. In that moment, as our bodies intertwined in a passionate frenzy, her husband approached from behind. My heart raced with excitement, wondering what he had in store for us next. Without warning, his finger slid into my eager anus, sending shockwaves of pleasure throughout my body. It was a sensation I had never experienced before—a delicious mixture of surprise and delight that left me craving more. Lost in this intoxicating dreamlike state, our desires entwined and boundaries blurred as we indulged our deepest fetishes together.

I made no attempts to stop him, of course. I was thoroughly enjoying the sensation of his finger inside me. As his finger delved deeper, my arousal grew stronger, powering my desire to engage with his wife even more passionately. The intensity of the experience was both exhilarating and surreal. Suddenly, he surprised me by shifting his attention to my anus, using his tongue to explore every inch of my ass. The pleasure intensified, causing me to release another soft moan of delight. It felt almost too good to be true, as if I were on the verge of climaxing all over his face. However, I resisted the urge to let go completely. I needed to hold back, proving that I was more than capable of fulfilling their desires and fantasies.

I couldn't believe what was happening, but I was determined to see it through. His tongue delved even deeper inside me, exploring every inch with an expert touch. With a sudden boldness, he spread my buttocks wider, granting him full access to my most intimate area. The sensation was overwhelming, and I found myself gasping for breath in pleasure and surprise. As his tongue penetrated my rectum, I felt a mix of sensations that sent shivers down my spine. It was a moment of pure ecstasy as he adeptly pleasured me, while his wife showered me with kisses on my neck, heightening the intensity of the experience.

After several seconds, he withdrew his tongue from my backside and sensually pressed his lips against my supple ass cheeks, as if he was paying homage to their divine curves. Meanwhile, I continued to passionately engage in carnal pleasure with his wife, our bodies intertwining in a whirlwind of desire. Suddenly, his hands firmly grasped my buttocks, forcefully parting them to expose my eager anus, primed for his exploration. With anticipation mounting, I felt the tantalizing touch of his throbbing six-inch member brushing against my trembling buttocks, teasing and testing the limits of my yearning hole. And then, without hesitation or resistance, he effortlessly plunged deep into the depths of my tight and welcoming ass, igniting a symphony of ecstasy that resonated through every fiber of our beings.

Taking his time, he pressed his hard cock inside of me, slowly penetrating me with deliberate precision. With each gentle thrust, he pushed deeper into my eager depths, before sensually withdrawing. The rhythm of his movements was intoxicating, a symphony of pleasure and desire. As he continued to explore the depths of my being, the intensity of the experience grew exponentially. It was an indescribable fusion of pleasure and vulnerability, a moment where reality blurred and only raw passion remained. This was not mere physical gratification; it was an awakening of the senses, a manifestation of our deepest fantasies coming alive in vivid technicolour.

I moaned in ecstasy, unable to contain my pleasure. His skilful prowess with his manhood was a divine revelation, a perfect match for my insatiable desires. The feeling of him deep inside me was overwhelming, as if I could explode with pleasure at any moment.

But I held back, appreciating every exquisite sensation without restraint. As he continued to thrust into me, the rhythm became more intense, igniting a fire within me that burned hotter with each movement. I reciprocated by intensifying my efforts with his wife, pushing her to new heights of ecstasy as well. The room filled with our combined moans and gasps, a symphony of passion and desire. Time seemed to blur as we lost ourselves in the primal dance of pleasure. My body quivered with excitement as the climax approached, building up like a tidal wave ready to crash upon the shores of our yearning.

In that moment of blissful abandon, my senses heightened and merged into a kaleidoscope of pleasure. My vision blurred as my eyes rolled back in sheer delight. Waves of euphoria washed over me, leaving me breathless and trembling from head to toe. I couldn't contain myself any longer; the desire to climax overwhelmed me, and I needed release right away. With a swift motion, I withdrew my throbbing member from his wife's tight embrace, spraying my hot essence across her ample 36C breasts. The sight excited her even more, igniting an insatiable hunger for my juices to cover every inch of her supple body. In that moment, her husband pulled out of me, his own arousal evident as he moved closer to his wife, stroking his length while fixated on our erotic display. Sensing the heat of the moment, I lowered myself beside her and watched with anticipation as she eagerly licked, sucked, and enjoyed every drop of my essence. Instructed by her passionate plea, I wasted no time in reciprocating the favour; hesitation was a foreign concept as I yearned to immerse myself fully in this decadent act. Yes, it was peculiar to taste my own cum, but the forbidden thrill sent waves of pleasure coursing through me until not a single drop remained unexplored.

Minutes later, her husband continued to indulge in the pleasure of sucking on her breast, relishing every moment as he relished the remnants of my release. There was an undeniable sense of satisfaction in his actions, a clear acknowledgement that he enjoyed the taste. Intrigued by their connection, I decided to join in, unsure whether they desired privacy or welcomed my participation in their passionate escapade. However, deep within me, an insatiable desire burned, rendering any thoughts of retreat impossible. I craved more; I yearned for an abundance of pleasure that seemed to be within reach. Succumbing to temptation, I boldly reached out and firmly grasped his throbbing shaft in my right hand, ready to explore uncharted territories.

"Would you like me to suck it?" I asked him with a seductive gaze, my desire evident in my eyes.

His response was immediate and resounding.

"Yes," but his desires went beyond just oral pleasure.

He craved the sight of his release splattering across my firm ass as I contorted myself to please him. Eager to fulfil his fantasies, I eagerly took his cock into my mouth, savouring every inch as if it were the most delectable treat. With each stroke of my tongue and every flick of my lips, I could sense his arousal intensifying. It was an exhilarating feeling, knowing that I held the power to bring both pleasure and release. And then it happened. The moment of ultimate satisfaction. His hot cum spilled forth, a testament to the pleasure we had shared. In that moment, I revelled in the knowledge that I had accomplished what few could—bringing two individuals to ecstasy in a single night.

But our adventure was not over yet. He desired more, pushing me to stand and bend over the dining room table. With legs spread wide apart, I eagerly positioned myself as he instructed. In a matter of seconds, his wife handed him a whip that she had been gripping tightly in her hands. She took pleasure in striking me repeatedly, and I cried out in agonizing pain with each lash. Being whipped was one of the most excruciating feelings I have ever experienced, but strangely, I didn't want it to stop. As each blow hit my skin, I became increasingly aroused. The sting mixed with an intense rush that sent shivers of both pain and pleasure through my body. After about seven strikes, she stopped and allowed her husband to tend to my wounds. He gently kissed my bruised flesh and rubbed it to ease the pain. His touch was both soothing and arousing, as if he knew exactly what I needed in that moment.

Eventually, his fat cock slid easily into my stretched sphincter and filled the void that had become familiar to me during the past hour. It was a bittersweet sensation; the pain from being whipped still lingered, but it was quickly overshadowed by the immense pleasure of feeling his cock thrusting inside me. He grabbed my sweaty hair and spoke dirty words into my ear as he fucked me with reckless abandon. I closed my eyes and surrendered to the intense pleasure of having his cock pounding into my asshole. To my surprise, his wife was still getting off on the whole situation; she sat on the couch playing with her pussy while her husband continued to pound into me. The room was filled with sounds of our moans and gasps, blending together in a symphony of passion.

It seemed like he was barely moving, just making small reflexive jerks with his hips, but it didn't take long for his cock to be fully buried inside me. We stayed still for a moment, locked together and frozen in pure bliss. The feeling of being filled by him was indescribable. Suddenly, I felt a rush as he reached climax and came inside my ass. I could feel waves of his hot cum filling me up and sending shivers of pleasure throughout my body. He pulled out shortly after and left me with a dripping, satisfied asshole on their dining room table. His wife wasted no time in diving in and licking up every drop of his sweet juice from my bum cheeks, her own moans mixing with mine as we both found our release.

I stood there in absolute amazement, my thoughts and dreams now a reality. The air was thick with cum, a palpable smell that electrified the room. I looked around me, taking in the scene of decadence and indulgence. Bodies intertwined, pleasure-filled moans filling the air, as taboo desires were unleashed without inhibition. It was a world where boundaries were shattered, where fantasies came to life. I couldn't help but be drawn in by the raw intensity of it all, feeling an unfamiliar heat coursing through my veins. In that moment, I knew I had found my place among these liberated souls, ready to explore every corner of pleasure's playground and ready to indulge in this fetish.

My First Crack

It was the first time that I ever tried crack,
A dangerous path that I knew I shouldn't backtrack.
The smoke filled my lungs, a burning attack,
A moment of weakness, a choice I now lack.

~

I felt its grip tighten, like a devilish pact,
The high was intense, but the aftermath exact.
My body trembled, my mind under attack,
Regret and fear consumed me, there was no turning back.

~

It's a seductive temptation, this addictive knack,
But I vowed to break free from its toxic impact.
No longer will I be held in its deadly clasp,
For my future and well-being, I will firmly grasp.

Eleven

Patrick

Looking back on it, I never thought that I was such a novel young bastard, a tantalizing human being, with a mind that craved forbidden desires. At the tender age of twenty-six, society expected me to possess some semblance of sensibility. Yet, in that particular moment, I understood my lack of restraint and embraced the depths of my carnal nature. And you know what? I haven't felt an ounce of remorse since. The feeling of exploring the uncharted territories of pleasure and indulging in the taboo has become an integral part of who I am—a thrilling deviation from the mundane norms that suffocate our existence. So yes, call me dirty or disgusting if you must, but I prefer to see myself as an exquisite enigma, an embodiment of passion and uninhibited exploration.

That night I wanted to experience a different kind of high, and I mean a mind-blowing, soul-awakening kind of high. So, without hesitation, I dialled up my friend Tanya and shared my intentions with her. Without missing a beat, she revealed that her parents had left for a weekend getaway, leaving us with the perfect opportunity to indulge in our desires without any worries. The thought of not having to sneak around or worry about getting caught sent a surge of excitement through my veins. After bidding Tanya goodbye on the phone, I wasted no time taking care of my hygiene rituals. I hopped into the shower, making sure every inch of my body was squeaky clean and refreshed. Once done, I swiftly dressed myself and stepped out into the night, ready to embark on an unforgettable journey into the realm of intoxicating bliss.

As I drove my car over to Tanya's house, all I craved was a night filled with exhilarating adventures and a carefree spirit. Tanya, my timeless companion, has been by my side since our early years, sharing secrets and creating unforgettable memories. Her youthful energy and compassionate nature always draw me closer to her. With anticipation building up inside me, I pressed the doorbell, eagerly awaiting her presence. The sound echoed through the hallway, and after a brief moment, she appeared at the door, radiating warmth and excitement.

"What's up, babe," I said with a playful grin, pulling her close for a warm embrace.

"Not much, Pat," she replied, her eyes twinkling mischievously. "I'm just about to take a steamy shower to wash away the stress of the day. But don't worry, I've already rolled us a joint, so feel free to indulge while I freshen up."

"Sounds like a plan," I chuckled, slipping off my jacket and kicking off my shoes.

I made myself comfortable on the couch, reaching for the freshly rolled joint. As the smoke filled the room and mellow tunes filled our ears, we lost ourselves in the haze of relaxation and desire. Our bodies intertwined, moving to the rhythm of passion and pleasure. As I sank into the plush couch, I ignited the pre-rolled joint and delicately positioned it between my lips. With a slow inhale, I drew in the potent smoke, relishing in its intoxicating embrace. The craving for a hit had been gnawing at me, leaving me restless for hours on end. With each exhale, my body surrendered to the soothing effects of the drug, releasing tension that had built up throughout the day.

Lost in my own haze of relaxation, a movement caught my eye. Tanya descended the staircase, adorned in a tantalizing ensemble - a short blue skirt that accentuated her shapely curves and a tight top that left little to the imagination. Tanya was known for her unabashed confidence and penchant for baring her skin, allowing it to breathe freely. However, my focus remained steadfast on the euphoric state induced by the weed coursing through my blood; her presence barely registering in my haze of blissful oblivion.

"You smoked all my shit already," she playfully remarked as she snatched the nearly depleted joint from between my lips.

I chuckled, amused by her quick reflexes.

"I didn't know you had such ninja skills. Did you just focus on your pussy and armpits while neglecting the rest of your body? Damn, Tanya, I've never seen a woman shower so swiftly in my life. Your pussy probably still smells like Coca-Cola and Burger King."

She smirked, taking a drag from the stolen joint.

"Well, if someone has my precious weed, you better believe I'll be moving at lightning speed. This ain't no free weed giveaway, honey."

We both burst into laughter, enjoying the playful banter and the shared sense of humour that bonded us together. In that moment, it felt like nothing else mattered except for the simple pleasure of being in each other's company and indulging in our favourite pastime.

"Anyway, listen babe, I got some new stuff that I've been itching to experiment with, and I know you're going to love it," she whispered seductively, her eyes sparkling with eagerness.

"What do you mean by 'something new'?" I asked, my curiosity piqued.

Her lips curled into a mischievous smile as she leaned in closer. "Jonny introduced me to this mind-blowing aphrodisiac, and as your adventurous partner, I thought we could give it a try tonight." My heart skipped a beat as the possibilities raced through my mind.

"Are you serious, Tanya? Do you really think it's a good idea?" I questioned, concern lacing my words.

She reached out and gently caressed my cheek.

"I know it can be intense, babe. But imagine the heightened sensations and pleasure we'll experience together."

My initial anger dissolved into a mix of excitement and apprehension. This was uncharted territory for us, but the allure of exploring new realms of passion was undeniable.

"Alright," I finally conceded. "Let's dive into this wild adventure together."

"Oh, stop it babe, it's only one hit," she pleaded, her voice filled with a mix of desperation and desire. "I promise I'll never try it again. We only live once, please," she added, her sad eyes searching for a glimmer of understanding in my own.

My heart raced as I considered her words. The fear of the unknown gripped me tightly.

"Damn, Tanya, I don't know about this," I confessed, my voice trembling with uncertainty. "What if I lose control? What if it changes me forever?"

She took a step closer, her hand reaching out to reassure me.

"You won't lose control," she assured me firmly. "We'll be there for each other every step of the way. Trust me."

As she walked towards the kitchen to prepare for our adventure, I couldn't help but to feel confused. This was uncharted territory for both of us - a forbidden journey into the depths of temptation. Taking a deep breath, I made up my mind. If we were going to take that leap together, we would face whatever consequences came our way - all in the name of living life to the fullest. At that point, I was already higher than a motherfucker, my heart pounding in my chest, and a sense of panic creeping in. The stories I had heard seemed like mere fiction until now; this was some serious fucked up shit.

As Tanya approached me, she held a coke can and a few other items tightly in her hands. It was surreal how quickly the atmosphere changed as she sat down in front of me. She started manipulating the can, creating a sizable dent in the centre and then puncturing a few more small holes. In that moment, it dawned on me that Tanya was no longer just a person I knew; she had transformed into someone entirely different. The way she handled the can with such precision and focus made me scared. I couldn't help but wonder what other hidden talents or secrets she possessed. The tension in the room escalated as Tanya continued her peculiar actions with the can. With each puncture she made in the can, it felt like I was witnessing a metamorphosis, a transformation that left me both mesmerized and terrified. My mind raced with questions, desperately seeking answers to make sense of this bizarre situation. Little did I know that things were about to take an even stranger turn, plunging me further into the depths of uncertainty and intrigue.

I wasn't certain about the exact number of holes she had pierced into the can, but it seemed to be around a dozen. With a flick of her wrist, she pulled out a cigarette from the box and scattered the ashes on the table. Then, she carefully positioned the cigarette ash over the dented spots where the holes were. Tanya proceeded to unveil a small crack and deftly broke it into two pieces using her bare hands. Slowly and meticulously, she used a knife to slice the crack into tiny fragments. Piece by piece, she delicately sprinkled the crack onto the can, ensuring that each fragment was placed precisely on top of the ashes. In just a matter of minutes, Tanya's dedicated efforts began to bear fruit.

Her crack can was ready to smoke, and I found myself captivated by the sight. My mind was racing with curiosity, but I couldn't find the words to express my amazement. It was as if she had mastered the art of smoking crack, effortlessly navigating through each step. The way she handled the can and lit it up revealed a level of familiarity that left me in awe. Perhaps she had experienced this before, honing her skills to perfection. There was no denying that what I witnessed was truly impressive; it seemed impossible to acquire such expertise without prior practice. As these thoughts raced through my mind, I couldn't help but acknowledge that she possessed a certain allure, a seductive charm that only added to the intrigue surrounding her crack smoking abilities.

"Damn, check out this masterpiece, babe. Look at what I just created," she exclaimed with a thrilling tone.

"It seems like you've got some serious skills, girl. You're totally rocking it over there, looking like a pro and everything. Just hope you're not getting into any trouble, Tanya. Your parents would flip if they found out," I warned playfully.

"Quit talking nonsense and come get a taste," she retorted, picking up the electric blue lighter that sat on the table between us.

With an air of confidence and mischief in her eyes, she flicked the flame to life and brought it close to her lips. She delicately placed the crack pipe between her lips, focusing on the small opening where one would typically take a sip. With a flick of the lighter, she ignited the substance and took a slow, controlled inhale. The smoke filled her lungs, seeping into every crevice, as she continued to draw it in until there was no trace of crack left in the pipe. Releasing her mouth from the makeshift vessel, she maintained a steady stream of smoke flowing through her nose, ensuring its potent effects were fully absorbed. As she exhaled, a sense of relaxation washed over her, causing her head to tilt back and rest against the plush cushions of the couch. Recalling Tanya's experience, it seemed that within just a few short minutes, her body would begin to crave more of this addictive substance.

"Do you want a hit of this?" she asked, her voice laced with a seductive allure.

Her eyes, glazed with desire, held me captive in their gaze. I hesitated, torn between my better judgment and the unknown. The scent that wafted through the room was different, like a forbidden fruit begging to be tasted. It was an aroma unlike anything I had ever experienced before, drawing me closer to the edge of temptation. With trembling resolve, I finally gave in to my curiosity and nodded my consent. Little did I know that this single moment would forever change the course of my life.

"Do you want a hit of this?" she asked, her voice dripping with seduction as she looked at me through hazy eyes.

The temptation was strong. I wanted to say no, to resist the intoxicating pull, but something inside me yearned for the thrill that awaited. With a trembling hand, I reached out and took the crack can from her weakened grasp. As I held it in my hands, I couldn't help but feel a mixture of fear and excitement coursing through my veins. I watched as the flame danced at the tip of the crack can, its flickering light reflecting in my dilated pupils. In that moment, time seemed to stand still as I prepared myself for what was about to come. Hesitation consumed me briefly before I made the decision to take that first inhale. As the smoke filled my lungs, a surge of energy rushed through my body like an electric shock. It was as if every nerve ending in my being came alive, igniting a fire within me that burned brighter than ever before.

In that single breath, I left behind all inhibitions and surrendered myself to the euphoria that awaited. The world around me blurred into a haze of pleasure and desire, leaving only sensations and cravings in its wake. My heart pounded in my chest with a primal rhythm, matching the intensity of this forbidden dance with danger.

But even amidst the rush and ecstasy, a part of me knew that this path was not sustainable. The addiction whispered its sweet promises while slowly tightening its grip around my soul. And yet, for now, I allowed myself to indulge in this novel experience, fully aware of the risks but unable to resist its seductive call. I felt an incredible sensation coursing through my veins. My mind was in a state of blissful tranquillity, as if time itself had slowed down to accommodate the euphoria. It was like floating on a cloud, my body completely at ease and relaxed.

In the midst of this surreal experience, a thought suddenly struck me like lightning.

"Did I really just smoke crack?" The realization hit me with such force that it sent shockwaves through my entire being.

My mind raced, grappling with the enormity of what I had just done. As I allowed myself to sink deeper into my thoughts, a profound weakness washed over me. With trembling hands, I carefully placed the can of crack on the table and attempted to close my eyes.

Every second that passed felt like an eternity as I tried to regain control over my senses. Suddenly, Tanya stirred on the couch beside me, her eyes displaying a faint glimmer of awareness. As she observed my state, a mischievous smile played upon her lips.

"Look at tiger over there with a hard on," she remarked, swaying back and forth in amusement.

The combination of emotions swirling within me was both thrilling and terrifying. It was as if I had entered into an alternate reality where pleasure and danger coexisted in perfect harmony. Tiger, Tanya's dog, was never the epitome of happiness, always barking incessantly about something or another. The constant noise grated on my nerves, making it difficult to find any peace of mind. And if the barking wasn't enough, Tiger had no regard for manners when it came to relieving himself - leaving his messes all over the house. It seemed that his lack of etiquette extended beyond just his bowel movements; his mouth was equally as uncouth. I found myself at a loss for words, unsure how to react to Tanya's bizarre behaviour. Minutes later, in disbelief, I watched as she knelt down beside her canine companion and proceeded to engage in an act that defied all logic and decency. Initially, I wondered if perhaps I had lost my sanity or if it was the drugs that was involved, but there was no denying what I saw. Tanya shamelessly performed a lewd act upon her dog right there on the floor.

I mean, was this not dog abuse? The thought crossed my mind as I witnessed the disturbing scene unfold before me. The sight was absolutely appalling, and I couldn't help but question whether it was necessary to intervene. Perhaps I should call animal control, I pondered to myself, feeling a mix of concern and disgust. This situation was truly beyond comprehension, and despite my inner turmoil, I found myself incapable of speaking up against it. My body seemed to betray me, freezing in place as a strange and unsettling sensation washed over me. It was a sickening realization that in some twisted way, I was becoming aroused by the act taking place right before my eyes. As Tanya continued her abhorrent actions, my gaze widened in shock and disbelief. She shamelessly took hold of the dog's minuscule member, bringing it to her mouth and engaging in an explicit act as if the dog were a human man.

I was utterly captivated as I witnessed the dog's eyes roll back and heard him groan in sheer excitement, completely taken aback by what unfolded before me. The next moment, she sauntered towards me with a mischievous smile, swiftly pulling down my pants, and without any warning, she commenced pleasuring me with her mouth. Yet, an overwhelming numbness had consumed my body, leaving me devoid of any control over the bizarre scenario that was unfolding. As she sensually sucked on my modest-sized manhood, it dawned on me in a moment of realization that this woman had just performed fellatio on her canine companion before turning her attention to me. The twisted nature of this situation left me astounded and questioning the depths of depravity I had stumbled upon.

Again, I found myself unable to resist her. With a deliberate and steady movement, I rose from my seat, guiding her gently to the edge of the couch. As her skirt lifted, revealing the tantalizing curve of her hips, I couldn't help but feel an eager anticipation building within me. Slowly, I lowered her panties, exposing her moist and inviting folds. It was in that moment that I realized my own size may not have been enough to satisfy her insatiable desire. Yet, rather than dwell on inadequacy, I embraced the challenge before me. Tanya's soft moans echoed in my ears as I explored every inch of her with my skilful tongue, determined to bring her pleasure beyond measure.

As I tugged on her silky hair and let my throbbing member plunge deep inside her, the only sound that reached my ears was the creak of a door being opened. Slowly, I pivoted my head to see who had intruded upon our passionate escapade. And let me fucking tell you, what transpired next would be etched in my memory for eternity. In that hazy moment, despite being under the influence, I managed to regain some semblance of control over my body. With a mix of fear and curiosity, I turned around and laid eyes upon an extraordinary sight - her family's dog's erect member still suspended in mid-air, the remnants of our drug-fuelled debauchery strewn across the table, and her parents frozen in utter disbelief. It was as if time had slowed down to capture this surreal tableau.

In that surreal moment, all we could do was stare at each other in silence, the weight of our actions hanging heavy in the air. The room seemed to pulse with a strange energy as we grappled with the consequences of our reckless desires. The look on their faces mirrored a potent cocktail of shock, horror, and confusion. I was on the verge of releasing my load inside her when the piercing sound of her father's voice shattered the moment.

"Michelle, GET MY FUCKING GUN!" he bellowed, his anger echoing through the halls.

In an instant, both Tanya and I sprang to our feet, adrenaline coursing through our veins. I can honestly say I have never moved so swiftly in my entire existence. It felt as if I were running not just from him, but from a future where my life had been cruelly cut short. As I dashed out of her house, fear gripping me tightly, visions flashed before my eyes - tearful mourners at my funeral, devastated loved ones who would never see me again. Everything became so vivid as I escaped with nothing but my pale skin and racing heart.

Needless to say, I never returned to Tanya's house again. After her father banned me from ever setting foot there, I couldn't help but reflect on the consequences of my actions. Was it worth it? Fuck yeah. The intense feeling of indulging in crack and engaging in passionate encounters was too intoxicating to resist. However, that experience served as a stark reminder of the dangers and addictive nature of such activities. While I made the conscious choice to abstain from that lifestyle, Tanya followed a different path, succumbing to the grip of addiction. It's unfortunate how one night can have such far-reaching consequences, forever altering the trajectory of our lives. And now crack, wasn't my fetish, but it was hers.

Fisting

She wanted me to fist her, twist her,
Turn her around and flip her,
Eat that pussy up from the back, then kiss her.

~

Frisk her, lick her, on that pussy as I dip her,
I might fuck that pussy, but I'll never ever miss her.

~

Risk her, lips her, play on that clit as I lift her,
Fuck her through the air as my hand pumps up in her.
Tease her, please her, make every inch of skin shiver,
Explore the depths of pleasure and deliver.

~

Caress her, undress her, ignite a fiery desire,
Take our passion higher and higher.
Seduce her, produce a symphony of moans and cries,
As we drown in pleasure beneath the starry skies.

Twelve

Mike

Okay, so I'm a browser. I love to sit in front of my computer and learn new things, and by new things I mean exploring different aspects of human sexuality. After delving into various online platforms, I stumbled upon a website called 'Seductive Secrets', a tantalizing online portal that promised to fulfil all my desires. Intrigued, I engaged in conversations with like-minded individuals and initially thought that it couldn't live up to the level of kinkiness I had encountered before. Little did I know how mistaken I was. The depths of passion and exploration that unfolded within the virtual realm were beyond anything I could have imagined. From steamy encounters to mind-blowing fantasies, 'Seductive Secrets' opened up a world of pleasure that surpassed my wildest dreams.

A young lady named Emma approached me, initiating a conversation that quickly delved into the depths of our most intimate desires and encounters. It was refreshing to find someone who shared my sexual interests and preferences. As we exchanged stories and fantasies, a certain electrifying connection began to ignite between us. Intrigued by her boldness, Emma decided to share a link with me, leading to a collection of her provocative online photos. Without hesitation, I eagerly clicked on the link, curious to explore this hidden side of her. As I perused through her pictures, I realized that Emma possessed a certain raw and unconventional beauty that transcended societal norms. I mean, sure, she wasn't drop-dead gorgeous, but beauty is subjective and what really mattered to me was the connection we had. As long as her pussy felt good and we had chemistry, that's all I cared about. I never judged a pussy based on its appearance - whether it was pretty or not, it didn't matter to me. What truly counted was that it was clean and well taken care of.

After our conversation, I couldn't wait to see her. I asked her to join me for drinks the following day, and she eagerly agreed. Emma was a woman who owned her sexuality without any shame or inhibition. She embraced her desires and wasn't afraid to explore them. It was refreshing to meet someone so open-minded and sexually liberated. The following day, we made plans to rendezvous at the Tesco's near my place. I know, it might seem like an unconventional choice for a meet-up, but hey, we weren't exactly looking for a fairytale romance here. We both understood the nature of our arrangement and had no illusions about it. As she approached me, I couldn't help but notice her bold choice of attire – a tantalizing red dress that barely grazed her thighs. It revealed her smooth, milky-white legs, giving me a glimpse of the effort she had put into shaving them. In that instant, I found myself hoping that she had taken the same care with her exquisite pussy.

As I approached her, I couldn't help but notice that she wasn't very pretty. Her short blond hair with a fringe did little to enhance her features. However, her choice of perfume was undeniably alluring. It was a scent that hinted at the possibility of an exciting encounter. We greeted each other with a tight hug, our bodies pressing against one another. In that moment, I could feel the suspense building up inside me. It was as if she knew exactly what I desired - her pussy clean and bare. The thought of indulging in some intimate oral pleasures sent shivers down my spine. As we arrived at my house, we drank wine and talked for what seemed like an eternity. Minutes later, she informed me that she was expecting a few friends to arrive later. Now, as open-minded as I am, I couldn't help but wonder why she hadn't mentioned this earlier. Did she think my place was some sort of wild sex party hub? Or maybe a secret underground club where people engage in all sorts of kinky activities? I mean, if her guests were into that kind of thing, it wouldn't bother me in the slightest. Perhaps they were just voyeuristic individuals who enjoyed watching others get down and dirty. Whatever the case may be, I was definitely intrigued by the possibilities that awaited us as the night unfolded.

I felt a mix of confusion and curiosity as I wondered if these individuals were robbers or rapists. It baffled me why I had invited this unattractive woman into my home, only for her to bring along someone else without giving me any prior notice. Despite my usual outspoken nature, I chose to keep my thoughts to myself and carry on with the evening. I was determined not to let her friends ruin my chances of getting intimate with her, so I decided to make a move and leaned in for a kiss, hoping to kickstart the night on a pleasurable note. After all, it seemed like the perfect opportunity to satisfy my desires before her friends made their presence known. Moments later, our bodies were pressed against each other, our lips locked in a passionate embrace. As my fingertips ventured lower, caressing her smooth skin, I could feel the heat radiating from between her thighs. The anticipation grew as I realized how eager she was for pleasure. With slow and deliberate movements, I slipped my hand under the fabric of her panties, feeling the slickness of her arousal against my fingers. A soft moan escaped her lips as I gently grazed her clit with my index finger. Our kisses deepened, our desire intensifying with each passing moment. And as I slid my middle finger inside her tightness, she arched her back in ecstasy, lost in the pleasure of our intimate connection.

I continued to playfully tease and withdraw, being mindful not to penetrate too deeply. My movements were focused on circling and dipping in and out of her luscious pussy, heightening her pleasure with each gentle touch. As our lips locked in an intense kiss, she began to sway her hips back and forth, craving even more stimulation. In response to her desire, I pressed my hand against her body, driving my fingers deep inside her wetness. The sensations overwhelmed her within seconds, and she unleashed a chorus of moans, hungering for even greater satisfaction.

"Oh yes, baby," she pleaded, "give me more. I need it."

After her fervent plea for more, I eagerly inserted three fingers deep inside of her velvety folds. With each thrust, I intensified my movements, delving deeper and applying more pressure to stimulate every inch of her sensitive walls. Sensing her heightened arousal, I positioned two fingers to maintain a steady rhythm inside of her while using the remaining digit to expertly tease and caress her swollen clit. Her moans grew louder as pleasure coursed through her body, and I could feel her wetness coating my fingers with each passionate stroke. As she writhed beneath me, lost in the throes of ecstasy, I decided to indulge in a slow and deliberate finger fucking, enjoying the way she quivered and tightened around me. Finally, unable to resist any longer, I plunged my fingers even deeper into her dripping core, pushing both of us to the brink of an explosive climax.

She reared up and shifted her body, gesturing her desire for more. Her moans grew louder as I continued to satisfy her with my skilled fingers. Sensing her craving for something more intense, she stood up and gracefully shed her little red dress. Climbing onto the bed, she presented her perfectly sculpted ass in the air, a seductive invitation.

"I want you to leave your mark on me," she whispered, her voice filled with a daring plea.

Intrigued by her bold request, I eagerly complied, sinking my teeth into the soft flesh of her ass. As I bit down, she let out a passionate cry, the mix of pleasure and pain fuelling her desire even further.

"Harder," she demanded, a hint of urgency in her voice. "Bite me harder."

Driven by an insatiable hunger to please her, I increased the intensity of my bites, leaving imprints of desire on both of her ass cheeks. Her intoxicating cries filled the room as our bodies intertwined in a frenzy of passion and exploration. As I withdrew my mouth from her left buttock, I noticed some slight discoloration on both of her gluteus maximus, evidence of my teeth leaving their mark on her fair skin. The sight only intensified my arousal, firing the desire coursing through my veins.

"Now," she commanded, delivering a firm smack to her right buttock, "I want you to eat my ass."

Eagerly complying, I rose to my feet and shed my garments, taking in the sight of her delicate figure nestled within my hands. With deliberate precision, I began by tracing circles with my tongue around the perimeter of her anus, teasing the sensitive edges while firmly grasping her cheeks. Immerse in the intoxicating scent and taste of her derrière, I continued to explore further, allowing my tongue to delve deeper into the velvety folds of her behind. The rhythmic motion of my oral ministrations elicited moans of pleasure from her lips as she arched her back in ecstasy. Lost in the realm of pure indulgence.

"Let me taste my ass, baby," she pleaded with a seductive look in her eyes.

Unable to resist her request, I withdrew my tongue from her delectable backside and proceeded to kiss her passionately. The sensation was unlike anything I had experienced before - an intoxicating blend of desire and pleasure coursing through my veins. As I delved back into her ass, the taste intensified, resembling a sinful combination of buttery sweetness and creamy decadence that made my taste buds tingle with delight. I eagerly continued my oral exploration, relishing every lick, slurp, and nibble as if it were the most exquisite delicacy. Overwhelmed by the intensity of our connection, I couldn't help but lift her body closer to mine, immersing myself even deeper in the act of pleasuring her.

"Oh, fuck yes baby, that feels so good," she cried out with enjoyment once again; I guess this was her favourite word.

"Your lips taste heavenly," I whispered in response. "I want you to explore every inch of my body," she moaned back.

With a sense of excitement, I trailed my tongue down her neck, savouring the salty sweetness of her skin. She arched her back in pleasure, urging me to continue.

As I moved lower, my mouth found its way between her thighs.

"I want to taste you," I murmured against her softness.

She gasped and spread her legs wider, eager for the sensation. Without hesitation, I delved into her wetness, using my tongue to tease and caress every sensitive spot. Her moans grew louder as I skilfully flicked and sucked on her clit. The taste of her arousal mingled with the sounds of our pleasure-filled symphony.

"No! I want your whole hand inside of me," she demanded, her voice filled with a mix of desire and urgency.

This request took me by surprise, as I had never explored such depths before. Uncertain but willing to achieve her needs, I approached cautiously, wanting to ensure her pleasure and comfort above all else. With a gentle touch, I began my journey by easing two fingers inside of her. As she moaned in response, I felt a surge of confidence. Gradually, I added a third finger, then a fourth, feeling the walls of her eager and accommodating pussy stretch to accommodate my hand. The sensation was overwhelming for both of us. As I slowly pushed my entire fist inside of her, she let out a mixture of pleasure and pain that reverberated through the room. It was an intense experience that pushed the boundaries of our connection, leaving us both breathless and satisfied.

I was convinced that I had ravaged her delicate folds, decimated her sweet spot, but to my surprise, this insatiable vixen continued to crave more. Her pussy clenched around my hand, adapting to its shape as if it were custom-made for pleasure. She clung onto the sheets, her eyes tightly shut, determined not to let a single moan escape her lips. In an attempt to alleviate the intensity, she grasped my left hand and squeezed it with passion. The mixture of pleasure and pain on her face only increased my desire to deliver even greater satisfaction.

"Are you okay, do you want me to stop?" I asked anxiously, my voice filled with concern.

"No baby, please I want more, give me more," she eagerly squealed, her desire evident in her voice.

I took a moment to pause and check in with her once again, making sure she was truly ready for what was about to come.

"Are you sure you are ready for this next level of pleasure, baby?" I asked, my tone filled with both anticipation and caution.

Her response was immediate and filled with a raw hunger.

"Fist me like no one else ever will," she moaned, her words igniting a fire within me.

As I looked at her lying there, craving every sensation possible, I couldn't help but be amazed by her uninhibited nature.

"Damn," I thought to myself, "this woman is a true sexual adventurer."

With no hesitation or doubt in my mind, I continued to complete her deepest desires. Gradually, as I entered her wetness, my hands found their place inside of her, exploring every inch, feeling the warmth and tightness that enveloped me. It was an intimate connection, a dance of pleasure. As I delved deeper, I sensed the pulsating rhythm of her body responding to my touch. With each movement, her inner walls embraced me, creating a symphony of sensations. Her voice filled the room with dedication and need, begging for more. The intensity grew as our bodies moved in sync, a primal rhythm that echoed through our beings. Moans and gasps mingled with whispered obscenities, heightening the passion that consumed us both.

"Oh, Jesus Christ baby, oh wow, YES, YES, FUCK ME" she yelled, her voice filled with a mix of pleasure and desperation.

I could feel her walls gripping my hand as I pushed it even deeper inside her. The intensity of her moans grew louder, matching the rhythm of my movements. I gaped at the tightness and warmth surrounding my hand, amazed by the depths she was willing to explore. As I rested my hand inside her for a few seconds, allowing her to catch her breath, I couldn't help but admire the power we both held in this moment. It was as if we were creating our own world of pleasure and desire. With each passing second, I became more aware of the forbidden territory that lay within her. And just when I thought there was no way back from this carnal journey, I teased her pussy by pretending to slowly withdraw my hand before plunging it back in with renewed force.

"Oh shit," she cried, then unexpectedly, I exerted my strength and withdrew my right hand from between her thighs with a forceful motion, a testament to the intensity of our encounter.

Her exclamations escalated as she yelled, "Ahhhhh, oh my fucking, shit hole, you motherfucker," her words mingling with the sounds of pleasure and ecstasy.

A smirk curled up on my lips as I basked in the satisfaction of my actions, feeling an incredible sense of empowerment surging through me. With her gasps for air filling the room, I couldn't resist but ask.

"Let me take you completely," as she arched her back slightly, immobilized by the overwhelming sensations coursing through her petite body.

About a minute later, she stood up and walked away from the bed, leaving me feeling confused and frustrated. What the fuck, man? First, you invite strangers into my own damn house, and now, after I just gave you the most mind-blowing pussy-eating session followed by an intense fucking, you want to bail on me? As I watched her retreat, doubts started creeping into my mind. Maybe that last move was too much for her. Perhaps I shouldn't have gone so hard. But then again, I've always been one to push boundaries and explore the depths of pleasure. Isn't that what great sex is all about? Going beyond societal norms and embracing our deepest desires?

But right now, all I could think about was how she left me hang-ing after all that passion we shared. The taste of her still lingering on my lips, the sensation of her body against mine etched in my memory. It was frustrating to be left in such a state of arousal without any release. She then walked over to the table where she had left her bag. As she made her way back towards me, my curiosity grew. I couldn't help but wonder what she had in that bag. Without hesitation, she tossed the bag onto the ground and pulled out a collection of erotic toys: handcuffs, a whip, and other tantalizing items. With a mischievous smile, she leaned in closer and whispered.

"Tonight, I want you to take control. Use these handcuffs to restrain me to the bed and ravish me until I'm begging for more. Remember, when I say 'deeper,' you go deeper. And if I tell you to stop... well, don't you dare stop."

The power dynamic shifted as she placed the handcuffs in my hands and sealed it with a passionate kiss. Seconds later, she gracefully positioned herself on the bed, spreading her limbs wide open in an inviting gesture. Her bare pussy was on full display, a mischievous grin playing upon its lips, enticing me to indulge in its pleasures. The air caressed her delicate skin, heightening the anticipation between us. As she lay there, vulnerable and eager, I restrained her hands and legs with gentle yet firm handcuffs, adding an element of thrilling submission to our encounter. With a wicked smile, I picked up the vibrating toy and approached her captivating form. Despite her outward appearance, her ass was surprisingly attractive, a sweet temptation that beckoned me closer.

Approaching her, I then knelt down below her pussy, staring at it as if we were in a face off. The suspense hung heavy in the air as our eyes locked, both knowing what was about to come next. With a devilish smile, I leaned in closer, my lips brushing against her delicate skin. Slowly, I traced gentle kisses along her inner thighs, inching closer and closer to her pulsating core.

Feeling the heat radiating from her arousal, I couldn't resist any longer. With a flick of my tongue, I made contact with her eagerly awaiting clit. Her hips bucked in response, urging me on. Taking the hint, I enveloped her sensitive bud with my mouth, alternating between soft licks and gentle sucks that sent shivers down her spine. As she moaned and writhed beneath me, I decided to add another element of pleasure. With a swift motion, I slipped two fingers inside her wetness, curling them just enough to find that sweet spot within her velvety walls. It wasn't long before she was gripping the sheets and arching her back, unable to contain the waves of ecstasy crashing through her body.

Knowing she was on the edge of release, I reached for a vibrating toy nearby and pressed it against her throbbing clit. The sensation intensified instantly, pushing her over the edge into a mind-blowing orgasm that left us both breathless and satisfied. The sensation of her toes curling and hair standing on end overwhelmed her as she felt the sweet vibrations pulsating inside her. The intense pleasure was heightened by the fullness in her core and the slight soreness between her thighs. With each passing minute, the flood of cum was released with even more force, followed by two minutes of continuous squirting onto the vibrator. As I knelt down closer, my mouth watered at the sight of her juices flowing out of her, eager to taste every drop. The refreshing sensation that washed over my body as I swallowed it down only powered my desire for her even more. Climbing on top, I teasingly rubbed my erect penis against her swollen clitoris, eliciting moans of pleasure from her lips.

"I need you right now, I want your big cock inside me," she begged, her eyes pleading for release.

Without hesitation, I entered her already wet pussy and thrust deep, appreciating the tightness and warmth surrounding me. She moaned with delight, smiling at me with an open mouth as I continued to thrust harder and faster at her request.

"Your eight-inch dick feels amazing, this is the best sex ever," she exclaimed.

Between gasps of pleasure as our bodies moved in perfect synchronization. This was pure ecstasy, a moment that neither of us would ever forget. Emma was primed for an intense experience, and that's precisely what she was going to receive. I launched myself onto her, eagerly exploring every inch of her body with my skilled tongue. With each flick and suck, I could feel her pleasure intensify, driving me to thrust deeper into her core. The sensations were overwhelming as waves of ecstasy washed over her, indicating the imminent arrival of her climax. Just as she was on the edge of release, a sudden interruption startled us both - the sound of the doorbell ringing. I reluctantly eased off my fervent penetration, giving Emma a moment to catch her breath and compose herself.

'Who the fuck could it be at this time of the night?' I wondered, irritation creeping into my voice. With a sigh, I hastily wiped my face clean with the bed sheets and threw on my dressing gown. The incessant ringing of the doorbell had pushed me to my limit. As I approached the door, a mix of curiosity and annoyance filled me.

'If it's not the police hunting down a murderer or a rapist, then they better have a damn good reason for disturbing me,' I muttered under my breath.

When I swung open the door, I was taken aback by the sight before me. Two men stood there, both dressed in gym clothes—one black and one white. A surprising wave of attraction washed over me as I took in their sculpted physiques. The black guy, in particular, caught my eye with his athletic build showcased by those tight gym shorts he was wearing. My mind raced with thoughts that were definitely not suitable for polite conversation. The air around us felt charged with an undeniable sexual tension. It was clear that these men weren't here for innocent chit-chat; something much more intimate was on their minds.

Trying to maintain some semblance of composure, I mustered a confident smile and asked.

"Can I help you gentlemen?"

"Hi, we are Emma's friends," said Mark. "She said it would be okay for us to drop by and chill out tonight." As I looked at Mark, I couldn't help but notice the confidence that exuded from him. It was clear that he wasn't shy, just like myself.

A smile formed on my face as I replied.

"Oh yes, she did inform me that you guys would be arriving soon. Come on in."

My heart raced a little as I led them into the living room, eager to hide the secret that lay behind closed doors. In that moment, a sudden realization hit me like a lightning bolt. Emma was securely handcuffed to my bed, her desires intertwining with mine. Panic washed over me as I hurriedly guided the two men inside, desperately hoping they wouldn't catch a glimpse of our private playtime.

As we settled into the cozy atmosphere of the living room, conversation flowed effortlessly. The air was charged with excitement and possibility; it was evident that tonight held more than just casual hanging out. Little did they know what awaited them once the night grew darker and our inhibitions were set free.

As the two men settled in, I guided them to the bathroom and graciously poured them each a glass of crisp white wine. Hurrying back to my bedroom, I couldn't help but notice Emma's pretty little pussy beckoning me once again, as if longing for my touch.

"Your friends have arrived," I informed her with a sly grin, suggesting we take a short break. "Would you care for a glass of wine?" I asked, trying to be polite.

"Yes, please," she replied coyly, her eyes fixed on me. With delicate precision, I released the handcuffs and poured her a glass of wine, our desires intertwining as we indulged in each other's intoxicating presence.

As we continued our conversation, Mark made his entrance into the room completely unclothed. I couldn't help but be taken aback by the sight of his impressive ten-inch member swaying freely before me. The rumours about black men and their well-endowed nature suddenly felt all too real as I found myself longing to taste him, to feel him deep in my throat. His naked, glistening body stood before me, and my eyes fixated on his throbbing manhood with a mix of anticipation and happiness. It was clear that he had been pleasuring himself in the shower, which only heightened my arousal even further.

"Sorry to interrupt, but I couldn't find a towel in the bathroom. Mind grabbing one for me?" he asked, his seductive gaze intensifying the tension in the room.

Before I could utter a word, Emma interrupted and said.

"Mike, this is Mark, and no, don't give him a towel, that impressive physique doesn't need to be covered up, it needs to be admired and celebrated. Mike, I want you to take charge of us, you have complete control over our pleasure, and I want you to revel in your dominance over us, so everyone can experience this ecstasy."

In that moment, my mind switched into overdrive. In my imagination, I transformed into a predator, ready to pounce on my target. And all I could see was that magnificent specimen of masculinity. Moments later, Dave sauntered into the bedroom, his body glistening with water droplets, completely exposed. As they both stood before me, a surge of confidence washed over me like a tidal wave. I felt like a seductive vixen who held the power to fulfil their deepest desires.

Without hesitation, Mark, Emma, and Dave dropped down onto their knees, presenting their firm asses and erect cocks. It was my turn to take control and show them the depths of my passion. With a hunger that consumed me, I sank my teeth into Mark's left ass cheek, relishing in the sensation as if it were the very essence of my existence. Mark exuded masculinity from every pore of his muscular body. Every inch of him was sculpted perfection begging to be devoured. I was unable to see his face as I bit his firm buttocks, but I could sense the arousal in his body as he tightly gripped his erect member and began to caress it with deliberate strokes. Eager to explore further, I traced my tongue along the sensitive skin of his anus, teasing and tantalizing him with each deliberate movement. Succumbing to the desire that pulsed between us, I pressed my tongue deeper into him, relishing in the taste and texture that engulfed my senses. As the intensity grew, I parted my lips and enveloped his throbbing shaft, savouring the sensation of it gliding against the roof of my mouth and down towards my eager throat. Though his buttocks were not as tight as anticipated, the pleasure they offered was just as exquisite and intoxicating.

I then moved over to Dave's pert little backside and nestled my face between his cheeks, indulging in the sensuous act of licking and teasing his delicate opening, coaxing it with my adroit tongue. The tightness of Dave's anus demanded a bit more effort on my part as I plunged my tongue deep inside, unearthing the hidden pleasures that awaited. His moans of delight only fuelled my determination as I fought against any reflex to gag, withdrawing momentarily before delving even deeper into him. With one hand expertly attending to his balls, I intensified the stimulation with my tongue, sending waves of ecstasy coursing through his body. It was then that I shifted my attention back to Mark's impressive ebony shaft, craving more of its taste and longing to feel its presence within me, but cautious not to let my desires overwhelm the moment.

I slowly and deliberately made my way towards him, anticipation building with every step. As I approached, I could feel the heat radiating from his body, expanding my desire. With a hunger that could not be contained, I took hold of his throbbing erection and guided it into the depths of my throat. The sensation was overwhelming, my throat muscles contracting and relaxing in rhythm as I worked to take him deeper. His moans of pleasure filled the air, rocketing my determination to please him even more.

Just as I thought things couldn't get any hotter, Emma's sultry voice broke through the haze of desire.

"I want to taste that ass," she declared, her eyes locked on the erotic scene unfolding before her.

In that moment, I withdrew from pleasuring him with my tongue and turned towards Emma, who lay on the bed with a look of intense longing in her eyes. Our lips met in a passionate kiss as we revelled in the taste of each other's desires. The room was filled with an intoxicating mix of lust and satisfaction as our bodies intertwined in a dance of pleasure. I stood up, a wicked grin playing upon my lips as I reached for the whip. It was time to explore new depths of pleasure, leaving delicious marks upon their willing skin. With each strike of the whip, their moans grew louder and their bodies writhed with ecstasy.

They were all lying on the bed, their bodies pressed against the soft sheets. As the dominant one, it was exhilarating to have them at my mercy once again. The power I held over their desires, their every whim and pleasure, sent shivers down my spine.

"Let the fucking show commence," I declared with a smirk.

With a swift motion, I cracked the whip and watched as it landed precisely on Mark's exposed flesh. The sound of his agonized cry filled the room, echoing through the air. It was a fierce blow, and I celebrated in the satisfaction of asserting my dominance. This wasn't going to be a gentle display; they would all experience the full force of my command.

"Did that hurt, baby?" I asked inquisitively, my voice dripping with eagerness. "I want to hear you scream, are you ready for this?"

My eyes gleamed with a wicked excitement as I slowly raised the whip high above my head. Without giving him a chance to respond, I brought it down with a resounding crack against his tender flesh. His reaction was immediate and intense.

"ARHHHH, my God, FUCK!" he bellowed, the pain and pleasure intertwining in his voice.

The marks from the previous blows were already starting to show on his beautifully dark skin, a testament to our shared desire for intensity. As he writhed and gasped for breath, I moved closer to Dave's tight white ass. The contrast of our skin only added fuel to the fire of our passion. Gently kissing his cheeks, I revelled in the taste of forbidden pleasure before once again raising the whip high above me.

With a swift motion, I brought it crashing down upon his back, delivering a powerful blow that sent shivers down both our spines. The air crackled with electricity as we delved deeper into our shared world of pleasure and pain. He was struggling to catch his breath and pleaded with me to cease, but I stood on my dominance. If he wanted any semblance of control in this performance, he would have to submit completely and feel every moment of it, speaking only when given permission. After delivering about ten powerful strikes, I allowed my aggression to subside slightly. Slowing down, I leaned in to kiss the marks left by the blows, relishing in the sight of Dave's bruised skin and red welts. This sight further aroused me, prompting me to drop the whip and forcefully guide his head downwards, spreading his ass cheeks apart as I thrust my cock deep into his awaiting hole.

I could hear his breath quickening and the soft, sensual sounds escaping his lips. His desire for me to penetrate him deeper was evident in the way his body arched towards mine. Without hesitation, I obliged, thrusting my member into his tight opening with a new-found urgency. The room faded away as our connection intensified, the pleasure consuming us both. His moans grew louder, harmonizing with the rhythm of our bodies as we moved together in perfect synchronicity. My insatiable hunger for him only intensified with every thrust, driving me to push deeper and harder.

"I want that big, thick cock," he moaned, his desire evident in his voice.

As I gradually slowed down and withdrew my member from Dave's tight hole, the anticipation grew. Moving towards Mark, I took control, gripping his head firmly and thrusting forcefully into him. The intensity of the moment was overwhelming, pushing me closer to the edge. Unable to hold back any longer, I felt my climax building rapidly. With each powerful thrust, pleasure surged through me until I couldn't resist any longer. In a matter of seconds, my release exploded inside Mark's eager ass, filling him with an undeniable ecstasy. Drip by drip, I allowed it to settle inside of him. Dave and Emma then knelt down onto the floor, their bodies hungry for more. They eagerly licked and drank my essence from Mark's ass, enjoying every drop as if it were the sweetest nectar. The room was filled with a symphony of moans and gasps, echoing the intensity of our adventure.

As I lay there, drifting between consciousness and blissful surrender, I couldn't help but marvel at the amazing scene unfolding before me. Emma and Dave, now driven by an insatiable hunger, turned their attention towards me. Their lips and tongues danced on my throbbing cock, sending waves of pleasure coursing through my veins. Meanwhile, Mark took his position behind me, his skilled tongue exploring every inch of my eager flesh. His expertise in pleasuring my most intimate regions left me breathless and craving for more. It was a moment where heaven and hell collided within me, igniting a fire that burned hotter than anything I had ever experienced before.

Amidst the passionate chaos, Emma's voice broke through the haze of pleasure. Her words sent shivers down my spine as she reminded me of our shared desire for dominance.

"You mentioned your desire to be dominated," she whispered seductively.

My heart raced at her words, the room grew even more electric with anticipation. We were all ready to delve deeper into the realms of ecstasy, pushing boundaries and surrendering to our deepest fantasies. I nodded in agreement, my voice barely audible as I watched her eagerly pleasuring me, her mouth expertly engulfing my throbbing member while traces of my release adorned her beautiful face. Her seductive tone urged me further as she commanded me to lie on the bed, promising an intense encounter. Surrendering to her dominance, I exposed myself completely.

Dave and Mark observed with rapt attention, their eyes fixated on the erotic scene unfolding before them. The room was filled with a palpable tension as Emma took hold of a whip, tracing its leather tendrils across my exposed flesh. Each strike sent waves of pleasure and pain rippling through me, heightening my senses and igniting an insatiable hunger within. In that moment, time seemed to stand still as the sound of the whip reverberated in my ears like a symphony of forbidden desires. The sensations overwhelmed me, transporting me to a realm where pleasure and pain intertwined in an inebriated dance.

This experience was truly unparalleled, surpassing any other encounter I had ever had in my life. If fate had decided to take me that very night, I believe even Jesus himself would have embraced me warmly. Perhaps with my cock still in my grip, but surely he would understand the depths of my passion. It goes without saying that Emma and I continued to cross paths on numerous occasions thereafter. She possessed an uncanny ability to unleash the darkest desires within me, unearthing a legion of demons that had long resided within. Without a doubt, she became my ultimate obsession, an embodiment of all my deepest fantasies.

Mile High

They call it skydiving, an exhilarating thrill,
But I was high and flying, my senses to fulfil.
As I soared through the air, weightless and free,
It felt like I was driving, in a world just for me.

~

And in that moment, a lover by my side,
My dick in her pussy, our passion did collide.
Like I was high and flying, our bodies intertwined,
The pleasure we shared, left no worries behind.

~

In this erotic dance, sensations ran deep,
My dick felt like I was crying, overwhelmed with heat.
Exploring each other's desires with fervent delight,
Our connection so intense, it felt just right.

~

So let's embrace the ecstasy that life can bring,
Whether skydiving or fucking, let's savour everything.
In moments of pleasure or soaring through the skies,
Let's indulge in the sensations that make us feel alive.

Thirteen

Eric

Skydiving had always been a thrilling adventure that I yearned to experience, so when the opportunity arose at the tender age of twenty, I eagerly seized it. The chance to embark on a tandem skydive for charity presented itself, and without hesitation, I completed the sponsorship forms, ready to dive headfirst into this adrenaline-fueled escapade. Through my relentless efforts, I managed to raise an impressive sum of over three thousand pounds, further fueling my anticipation for the impending leap. Excitement coursed through my veins as I received the long-awaited date for the skydiving extravaganza, only to realize that it fell on a Sunday.

However, fate had a different plan in store for me as I found myself DJing in a lively club until the early hours of Saturday morning, leaving me with little time to rest before embracing the exhilarating plunge into the unknown. Speed, or amphetamine, was something I was heavily into at the time and I even used it when playing in football matches to give me an extra edge. It helped me concentrate and kept me awake. So naturally, when Saturday evening rolled around, I indulged in a few lines of speed to keep me going. The pulsating beats of the underground techno night awaited me at the club nestled beneath the railway arches.

As the music enveloped my senses, the rush of energy from the amphetamine coursed through my veins, heightening my experience on the dance floor. The combination of mind-altering beats and amplified focus fueled by speed created an electrifying atmosphere that transcended mere entertainment. It was as if each beat synchronized with the pounding of my heart, propelling me into a state of euphoria where inhibitions were shed and pleasure reigned supreme. By the time everything was winding down in the club, the sun had already begun to rise, casting a warm glow over the city streets. As the last notes of the final song faded into the early morning air, I carefully packed up my equipment, feeling a mix of exhaustion and exhilaration from the night's performance. With my record box securely in hand and headphones draped around my neck, I made my way towards the exit, ready to embark on a new adventure. Outside, I found my car waiting patiently, its engine humming softly as if eager to hit the open road. Excitement bubbled within me as I climbed into the driver's seat, joined by three close friends who were equally eager for what lay ahead. Together, we embarked on a journey that would take us to an airfield nestled amidst rolling hills and endless skies - our destination for an unforgettable skydiving experience.

The excitement was growing as I pulled my car into the designated jump area, but it was only the early hours of the day, allowing us some time to kill. With the sun shining brightly and a warm breeze flowing through the open car doors, we cranked up the music on the stereo, immersing ourselves in its pulsating beats. In the backseat, Bob and his girlfriend Sue were engaged in some illicit activities, meticulously dividing lines of cocaine on record sleeves.

To my surprise and delight, they generously offered me a share of their indulgence, passing over a line for me to snort alongside them. Initially, I had thought it was speed, or amphetamines, as Sue, a very intelligent and attractive lady who worked for the probation services, she was also a crazy phet-head who started her day off with a teaspoon of speed. The smell, or lack of it, told me otherwise straight away. My eyes grew a little wider as I realized that what was being passed to me was not what I expected. It wasn't the familiar scent of amphetamines, but rather the unmistakable aroma of marijuana. As I took a drag from the joint that was handed to me, a wave of relaxation washed over my body. The high began to take hold, and I could feel my mind drifting into a state of blissful euphoria. Despite the initial confusion, this unexpected twist in substances turned out to be a pleasant surprise, offering a different kind of escape from reality.

During the next couple of hours, as we anxiously awaited my jump, the four of us indulged in roughly five grams of cocaine. The effects were undeniable; I felt an overwhelming sense of invincibility coursing through my veins. My senses were heightened, and my nose, lips, and mouth were completely numb from the constant snorting. Occasionally, I would experience drop backs, where the congealed cocaine from my nostrils would slide down my throat. Thankfully, I always had Airwaves chewing gum to assist in dislodging any remnants. In fact, I discovered that mixing the cocaine with the gum allowed it to enter my bloodstream through my gums, providing an even more intense high.

So, it was a stunningly beautiful day, the sun shining brightly overhead as I stood there with three close friends. As we gathered together, I couldn't help but feel a delicious tingling sensation coursing through my entire body. It wasn't just anticipation that had me buzzing; it was the lingering effects of the wild night before, and the thrill of what awaited us. With wide eyes and an electric energy pulsating within me, I confidently approached the registration office and handed over all the necessary paperwork. The rush of adrenaline mixed with the remnants of cocaine in my system only intensified my senses as I eagerly signed the insurance waivers. Soon enough, we were directed to a briefing area where a group of fellow daredevils awaited us, all ready to dive into this exhilarating adventure together. Each of us in the briefing was clearly excited, but I was absolutely fucking buzzing. The adrenaline coursing through my veins made me feel alive, like I could conquer the world. I had to restrain myself from bouncing off the walls or screaming at the top of my lungs. The feeling was intoxicating, powering my every move and thought. It was as if I had a secret power, a hidden energy that propelled me forward.

The instructors led us to a staging area in a hangar where we all picked out jumpsuits and met the person we would be doing our tandem jump with. Excitement filled the air as we geared up for the thrilling adventure ahead. Finding a jumpsuit that fit perfectly proved to be a challenge, but I eventually found one that hugged my body just right. It was sleek and black, giving me an edgy look as I prepared for the dive of a lifetime. The anticipation grew as I stood there, surrounded by fellow adrenaline junkies ready to conquer the sky. We exchanged nervous glances, knowing that in just a few moments, we would be soaring through the air at unimaginable speeds. The energy was electrifying, increasing our desire for an unforgettable experience.

Soon we were shown the plane we would jump from, as we were led outside to the runway. Stepping inside the aircraft, we settled into our seats with our legs spread apart, side by side, feeling the adrenaline pumping. The anticipation was electric as we fastened our harnesses and prepared ourselves for the ultimate thrill. As the plane ascended into the sky, I couldn't help but marvel at the breathtaking view unfolding before my eyes. The vast expanse of blue stretched out infinitely, enticing us to embrace its freedom and adventure. This wasn't like any plane I had ever been in before. It was a single engine propeller plane, stripped down to its bare essentials. Inside, there were no plush seats or luxurious amenities. Instead, the cabin was sparse and utilitarian, with only enough space for the pilot and co-pilot to sit comfortably. Even the door itself was unconventional, resembling more of a makeshift cover than a traditional aircraft entrance. It was made of corrugated plastic, extending downward from the top of the plane, reminiscent of the shutters on a shop front.

As we barrelled down the runway, the deafening drone of the engines filled my ears. Glancing over at Bella, one of my fellow tandem jumpers, I could see a mix of excitement and nervousness playing across her face. It was clear that the reality of what we were about to do - hurtling towards the ground from fifteen thousand feet - had finally set in. She smiled at me, but not just any smile, a very seductive smile that made my balls tingle. Igniting a fire within me, I couldn't help but imagine what pleasures awaited us. As the plane's undercarriage lifted off the ground, I felt a surge of excitement coursing through my veins, matching the adrenaline rush of skydiving itself. The feeling of the unknown merged with the primal desire within me, creating an intoxicating mix of fear and arousal. With each passing moment, our bodies pressed closer together, as if gravity itself was pulling us towards an inevitable collision. As we soared through the clouds, our passion reached new heights, intertwining in a dance of ecstasy that defied logic and reason. In that exhilarating moment, I knew that this weekend would be etched into my memory forever.

As the plane continued to ascend, my ears felt the increasing pressure and began to pop. The exhilarating sensation was heightened by the occasional shouts from the midget strapped to my back. Despite not understanding his words, I responded with a nod or a thumbs up, eager to show my enthusiasm. Soon enough, we had reached the designated altitude for our jump, and the rear door of the aircraft was opened. The rush of wind filled the cabin, amplifying the excitement within me. Observing closely, I watched as the first pair of jumpers leaned forward and disappeared into the vast expanse below. Now, there were only two of us left: myself and Bella. It was finally her turn to take the leap of faith into the open sky.

You could tell that she was under the influence; her bloodshot eyes and unsteady gait were dead giveaways. Slowly, she rose from her seat and made her way towards the plane's exit. Standing there, she seemed lost in thought, contemplating her next move. In that moment, I couldn't help but be captivated by her unpredictability - it was like a scene straight out of a thrilling novel. As if on cue, Bella approached me and locked eyes with me, an intense connection forming between us. Without uttering a word, she leaned in and kissed me passionately. The electricity between us was evident. Then, without warning, she retrieved a pocketknife from her pocket and cut a hole in my pants, revealing my desire waiting to be unleashed.

As she took my cock out, her mouth enveloped it with a voracious hunger that made me shiver in pleasure. I couldn't help but lean back, overwhelmed by the intensity of her oral skills. It was as if she had mastered the art of giving head with unparalleled passion and expertise. In that moment, I realized that skydiving wasn't the only adrenaline rush I craved; her relentless sucking had ignited a fire within me that could only be extinguished by fucking her. With each rhythmic motion of her tongue and lips, my desire to explore the depths of her wetness intensified, driving me to the brink of ecstasy.

Minutes later, she released my throbbing member from her mouth and gracefully straddled me. Her legs tightly encircled my waist, ensuring a firm connection between our bodies. The sensation of her drenched pussy enveloping my hard cock sent shivers of pleasure coursing through me. Our bare skin pressed against each other, igniting a primal desire within us both. It dawned on me, in the midst of my intoxication, that Bella had orchestrated this encounter with meticulous precision. The strategic opening she had prepared in her delicate folds left no doubt that she was well-versed in the art of seduction.

As I dangled my legs out of the plane, the bright blue sky stretched out in front of me, the wind blasting onto my numb and tingling face. Peering out at the amazing expanse, I couldn't help but feel a surge of excitement mixed with a touch of fear. But then she leaned in closer, her body pressed against mine, and everything else faded away. With expert precision, she started to move her hips in a rhythmic motion on my waist, each movement sending waves of pleasure through my body. Using her hands, she skilfully secured my throbbing dick inside of her, intensifying the sensations coursing through me. A loud moan escaped my lips as I surrendered to the overwhelming pleasure that consumed me in that moment. It was a perfect blend of adrenaline from the impending skydive and pure ecstasy from this intimate connection.

The horizon seemed to stretch out endlessly, a vast expanse that filled my senses with wonder. As Bella and I approached the edge, I couldn't help but feel a surge of adrenaline coursing through me. The world below, once sprawling fields now reduced to miniature patches of green, added an element of surrealism to the moment. Just as we prepared for the exhilarating plunge, a sudden rush of vertigo overwhelmed me. The spinning and tumbling blur turned everything into a chaotic dance of sensations. In that dizzying whirlwind, there was no correct pose to maintain, for Bella unleashed her passion upon me with even greater intensity. The grinding and bouncing became a symphony of pleasure that echoed through the air, defying gravity itself.

Thousands of sensations rushed through my mind and body, accentuated by the copious amount of cocaine in my system. This heightened state of euphoria propelled me to new heights, both figuratively and literally. As we hurtled through the sky, the adrenaline coursing through my veins intensified the rush, amplifying every sensation. The wind whipped against my face, competing with the exhilarating thrill that consumed me. In this moment, I felt truly alive, liberated from the constraints of everyday life. The camera-wielding skydiver approaching us only added to the intensity, capturing every heart-pounding second as we descended towards earth at breakneck speed.

When I reviewed the footage afterwards, it dawned on me just how absurdly wide my grin appeared. The sheer force of the wind, hurtling past at breakneck speeds of a hundred and twenty-five miles per hour, made my face contort in a comical manner. It was akin to the way your mouth stretches open when you stick your head out of a car window on the freeway. But in my case, the mixture of numbed gums from indulging in copious amounts of cocaine and the exhilaration of being fucked mid-air only intensified my euphoria. It was as if every sensation was amplified, merging pleasure with adrenaline in an electrifying symphony that left me craving for more.

While we were only in freefall for a brief forty-five seconds, it felt like an eternity of exhilaration. The rush of wind against my face and the adrenaline coursing through me made every second feel stretched out, intensifying the experience. As the thrilling descent continued, a sudden tap on my shoulder jolted me back to reality; it was time to deploy the parachute. It was then that I became acutely aware of Bella strapped onto my body. Following the instructions from the pre-jump briefing, I crossed my arms tightly in front of my chest, ensuring her safety and mine. With a quick release, the parachute opened, abruptly halting our rapid descent from one hundred and twenty-five miles per hour to an almost instant standstill in just three exhilarating seconds.

The sudden jolt shook my head, and everything went from a frenetic, noisy, horizontal rush to a serene, almost silent calm as the both of us dangled from a giant sheet and gently drifted towards the ground. With all the various natural and artificial sensations coursing through my body, the last two minutes of our descent felt like an otherworldly experience. Time seemed to stretch and warp, as if we were suspended in a dream-like state. As we neared the earth below, the world became more defined, every detail standing out with an extraordinary clarity. The pressure in my head lingered from our daring plunge from fifteen thousand feet, yet it was overshadowed by the pulsating exhilaration that coursed through my blood. It was as if my mind had been transported to another realm where boundaries ceased to exist and pleasure took on new dimensions.

Consequently, we found ourselves touching down in a cabbage field situated at a considerable distance from the airstrip. Our landing was accompanied by a jolt, and we were subsequently dragged along the ground for a short distance. Yet, despite the rough landing and subsequent dragging, I remained unfazed by the situation. I don't think I would've given a damn even if my legs were shattered at that moment. The rush from the cocaine, mind-blowing sex, and heart-pounding adrenaline was still coursing through my veins, leaving me grinning from ear to ear. Suddenly, a person associated with the airfield sprinted over, accompanied by the cameraman who had taken the leap with us. With trembling legs, I unfastened myself from the tandem harness and struggled to stand upright; my throbbing member proudly erect for all to witness, making it difficult for me to maintain balance.

I was left in awe, not because I was injured, but because of the intoxicating cocktail of drugs. The sensations were electrifying, a wild symphony of pleasure and exhilaration. Looking back, it's a wonder I didn't lose all control as the drugs collided within me. Meanwhile, Bella composed herself with remarkable speed, as if our mid-air escapade was just another casual encounter. She sauntered off to prepare for the next adventure. As I replayed the video later, I couldn't help but notice the skydiver's somewhat resentful expression. Yet, in that moment, I was far too consumed by my own sensations to truly care. The rush of adrenaline and the effects of cocaine had me in a state of complete euphoria. If a cow had approached me after landing, I would have likely showered it with gratitude. My ears were still adjusting from the intense jump, causing all sounds to be muffled, while my eyes felt like they were going to burst out of their sockets. It was as if the entire experience had taken me to new heights of pleasure and excitement.

After getting back to the hangar, I quickly stripped out of my black polka dot jumpsuit, now sporting a massive hole in the crotch area. With a mix of exhilaration and exhaustion, I made my way towards Bob, Bella, and Sue, our fellow skydiving enthusiasts. The adrenaline rush was slowly dissipating, but a lingering sense of thrill still coursed through my veins. As we gathered around, swapping stories and reliving the heart-pounding moments we had just experienced, I couldn't help but notice the mischievous glint in everyone's eyes. It was clear that the adventure had sparked something wild within all of us. With our hearts still pounding from the rush of freefalling through the sky, we laughed and joked, savouring the taste of danger that lingered on our lips.

Bob kindly offered to take the wheel as I was starting to tremble slightly, though I couldn't pinpoint whether it was due to the rush of adrenaline, the lingering effects of our passionate encounter, or perhaps a combination of both. As we departed from the airfield parking lot, we had barely covered half a mile when exhaustion overwhelmed me, causing me to drift into a deep slumber for the remainder of the journey. It wasn't until we arrived at Sue and Bob's house that Bella and I continued our passionate escapade, exploring each other's bodies with fervour until I reached my climax inside her velvety folds. Undoubtedly, this was one of the most exhilarating moments in my entire existence. Now, was it my fetish? Sorry, but I don't kiss and tell.

Candaulism

As he pleasured me with his tongue, I felt a voyeur's gaze,
Another man watching, adding an erotic haze.
The combination of sensations had me in a daze,
Calming and sexy, my mind was ablaze.
His oral skills were impeccable, my pleasure he did raise,
And with each lick and suck, my body gave praise.

~

The intensity grew as I neared ecstasy's brink,
Both men's eyes locked on me without a blink.
It was a thrilling sight, making my heart sing,
Having them both witness the pleasure I bring.
With every stroke and touch, they made my body zing,
A symphony of desires, our passions taking wing.

~

As his mouth worked its magic on my most intimate place,
The air filled with moans and the scent of pure grace.
I could feel the heat rise, spreading at a steady pace,
My body responding to his every embrace.
The pleasure intensified, leaving no empty space,
I surrendered completely to this sexual chase.

~

In that moment of connection, nothing else mattered,
The world around us faded as our desires shattered.
Two men indulging in fantasies that left us scattered,
Exploring boundaries that society deemed taboo and battered.
It was an experience that left us all feeling flattered,
An unforgettable encounter that our memories forever
treasured.

Fourteen

Charlotte

To be completely honest, I couldn't quite put my finger on it, but there was something about him that made me crave a transformation. From the very moment our paths crossed, I sensed his potential for growth and his willingness to fulfill my every need Deep down, I knew he possessed the skills to pleasure me like no other, as if he could devour my essence with a single touch. Yet, I understood that this kind of expertise takes time to cultivate.

That night we went out to eat, indulging in a delicious meal that set the tone for a memorable evening. The atmosphere was intimate, and we appreciated every bite as we shared laughter and deep conversations. Our connection grew stronger as we expressed our desires and fantasies, teasing each other with whispered promises of pleasure to come. In my mind, images of his lips on my body danced provocatively, igniting a fiery anticipation within me. The thought of him exploring every inch of my skin with his tongue sent shivers down my spine. Reality had a way of sometimes surpassing even my most vivid imagination. As we stumbled through the front door of his house, our intoxication only heightened the intensity between us. I knew exactly what lay ahead, so I took the time to pamper myself in preparation. A long shower left me feeling refreshed and ready for the wild adventure that awaited us. With freshly shaved legs and a perfectly groomed body, I laid on the bed, eagerly waiting for him to join me. The air crackled with electricity as he emerged from the bathroom, his eyes filled with desire.

I observed intently as he strolled across the room, stripping off his t-shirt and pants. Within moments, he exited the space, likely heading for a refreshing shower. As he left, my excitement grew knowing that it was my turn for some pleasure. Eagerly spreading my legs wide, I decided to prepare my pussy for his arrival. With my index finger, I began to tease my vagina gently, sliding in and out repeatedly. Gradually, I could feel myself getting more aroused, my body awakening to the sensations as my eyes rolled back in sheer ecstasy. Now, with my middle finger delicately rubbing my clit, I awkwardly spread open my pussy lips with the fingers on either side.

I was incredibly aroused, my wetness causing my fingers to struggle in finding the exact spot on my clit. It was a delicious challenge, as my digits slipped and slid over every inch of my sensitive flesh. With each touch, I delved deeper into the intricacies of my own pleasure, exploring and investigating my pussy with a fervent curiosity. My fingers danced with purpose, teaching my kitty a valuable lesson in ecstasy. Just as I prepared to release my desires all over his bed, he unexpectedly entered the room. A mischievous grin adorned his face as he casually wiped away any evidence from his encounter with me.

"You're already indulging in her delights?" he playfully questioned, his voice laced with anticipation.

I then smiled at him, not uttering a word, just simply observing his every move as the towel slipped from his waist and revealed his erect manhood. His penis appeared firm, yet enticingly pliable, an invitation to explore the depths of my pleasure. With a confident stride, he approached the couch and settled himself down, fixated on the spectacle before him as I indulged in mind-blowing orgasms that drenched his luxurious bed. After a captivating ten minutes of watching me pleasure myself, he could no longer resist the allure and desire coursing through his veins; he hungered for a taste of the action that awaited him.

He then approached me and positioned himself below my pussy, fixating his gaze upon it, his mind filled with curiosity, contemplation, and even a hint of overthinking. Completely caught up in the moment, he tenderly inserted his middle finger inside of me, skilfully fingering me in a rhythmic motion. Moments later, he sensually brought his finger to his mouth, enjoying the taste and indulging in the sensation of licking and sucking on his own digit. This pleasurable act continued for several minutes as he satisfied his desires. Adjusting his position slightly, he proceeded to repeat these tantalizing actions with me once again.

Now, with his fingers deep inside my wet and eager pussy, he allowed me to taste the essence of our passion. I delighted in the delicious tang of my own desire, relishing each decadent drop as if it were a rare delicacy. It was like a tantalizing blend of sea salt and sweet nectar, a taste that transported me to a tropical paradise where pleasure washed over me in waves. For twenty glorious minutes, he adeptly explored the depths of my craving, plunging in and out with an expertise that left me trembling and yearning for more. But despite his carnal prowess, he hadn't yet indulged in the intoxicating act of licking and sucking my throbbing clit.

I could feel the anticipation building within me, a hunger that begged to be satisfied. As his fingers continued their relentless dance within me, I couldn't help but wonder when he would finally give in to the insatiable craving burning between my thighs. But I knew patience was key. Great pleasure awaited us both once he unleashed his oral skills upon me, taking me to heights of ecstasy I had only dreamed of. So, I eagerly waited for the moment when he would lower himself between my legs and feast upon my pulsating core, driving me wild with pleasure beyond imagination. He had never engaged in the pleasurable acts of licking, sucking, or allowing any woman to face rape him before, and it took him a few months to succumb to my irresistible allure. How did I manage to captivate him, you may wonder? Well, because I possess an undeniable confidence and assertiveness that can only be described as badassery. I didn't shy away from making suggestions; after all, a woman should never hesitate to express her feelings. Honesty is key in any relationship, so I made sure he knew exactly how I felt. Trust me, I've learned from past experiences that without open communication, a connection is doomed to fail time and time again.

But with him, my suggestions transformed into a thrilling reality and he flawlessly grasped, interpreted, and fulfilled my deepest desires. In the midst of his dexterous finger fucking, a persistent knock echoed at the door. Anticipation coursed through me; I knew exactly who it was and what awaited us. With one last passionate kiss, he gracefully rose from the bed and composed himself. Making his way to the chair, he effortlessly draped his robe around his sculpted physique before answering the door. Meanwhile, I remained exactly where I was – legs spread wide, my bare pussy eagerly exposed, prepared and yearning for the impending ecstasy that was about to unfold.

As he swung open the door, his friend's voice echoed through the room. It was clear that they were up to something exciting. And well, this is where I feel it's only fair to give you all the full story. As I mentioned before, it took some time for him to fully satisfy my desires. I wanted him to truly understand what pleases me, so I suggested he do some research and explore different techniques. We even watched some explicit movies together, using them as inspiration for our own intimate adventures. The agreement we reached was unconventional but thrilling - he would find someone skilled in the art of pussy eating, and I would let him watch as they indulged me in breakfast, lunch, and dinner delights. It may seem unconventional to some, but for us, it was a way to explore and expand our sexual horizons together. After all, why should he learn on his own when we can both enjoy the experience?

This was a first for me, as adventurous as I am in the bedroom. Initially, I felt a twinge of nervousness, but I quickly suppressed it and embraced the excitement coursing through my veins. The suspense was akin to standing at the edge of a precipice, ready to dive into uncharted territory. As his friend stepped into the room, the atmosphere electrified with an undeniable sexual tension. It felt like we were participants in an explicit film, ready to push boundaries and explore our deepest desires. You see, my possessive boyfriend had forbidden any interaction between this man and me; all he craved was for him to orally pleasure me before disappearing from our lives. And believe me, I had no objections whatsoever. As his friend entered the room, shedding his jacket and then gracefully removing his shoes, he finally began unveiling the tantalizing possibilities that awaited us.

Seconds later, his shirt slid off his sculpted torso, revealing the chiselled muscles that lay beneath. It was a bold move, considering we had agreed not to engage in any sexual activities. But perhaps he couldn't resist the temptation that lingered between us. As he stood before me, shirtless and confident, I couldn't help but admire his audacity and the way his eyes sparkled with desire. Although there would be no fucking tonight, the hope of exploring each other's bodies still hung heavily in the air. And as I looked into his eyes, I knew that even without penetration, our encounter would be nothing short of electrifying.

As my boyfriend settled onto the couch, still clad in his robe, his friend approached me with an air of courtesy. It was as though he understood the boundaries and didn't want to overstep them. He moved cautiously, avoiding any areas that were off-limits. Without uttering a single word, he lowered himself to his knees while I lay on the bed, contemplating whether I should really go through with this. There was no turning back now; I had made up my mind. My legs trembled in preparation as I grappled with the idea of another man's hands on me. I didn't even know this guy; what the hell was I thinking?

As I was about to lose myself in my own thoughts, I suddenly felt the sensation of his cool, substantial lips delicately caressing my most intimate area. In that moment, all of my doubts and uncertainties simply vanished into thin air. With just one kiss, it felt as if all of my emotional wounds had been miraculously healed; my mind became crystal clear and I was overcome with a newfound confidence to conquer anything that came my way. He continued to skillfully explore every inch of my vulva with his tender kisses, evoking a sense of pleasure that left me speechless. To be honest, I was unsure how to respond; the fear of moaning too loudly and arousing suspicion from my boyfriend lingered in the back of my mind. But there was no way I was going to let this incredible experience go to waste; I was determined to savor every moment for as long as it lasted.

I started off slowly, savoring every moment as his lips danced to the rhythm of my body. The sensation of his wet kisses cascading over my most intimate parts was pure bliss, as if he had been born to please me in this very way. It was clear that he possessed a deep understanding of pleasure and knew exactly how to deliver it. In a matter of seconds, his hands skillfully parted my delicate folds, and I could sense that my world was about to be forever changed. With gentle precision, his fingers explored the outer contours of my throbbing center, prompting me to open myself even wider. I eased back, allowing him deeper access, relishing in the exquisite sensation as his fingers slid inside me, igniting a fire that consumed every inch of my being.

As the anticipation built, I couldn't help but release a passionate moan. With each gentle push, he delved deeper inside me, exploring the depths of my inner lips. Being well-acquainted with my own body, I knew the intricacies of every part, and he was now experiencing the full extent of my pleasure. His tongue expertly traced every inch of my pussy, provoking an uncontrollable surge of lubrication that cascaded onto his lips. You see, I possessed the ability to squirt, so if I wasn't gushing with pleasure, my pussy remained in a perpetual state of readiness for either fucking or oral stimulation. It was this constant wetness that powered our lust-filled encounters.

As my body took shape, I could sense that he had a delicious blend of my wetness and his saliva swirling in his mouth. The excitement grew as I knew his face was about to be engulfed by the tidal wave within me. With a seductive smile, I uncovered my throbbing core, eager to witness the ecstasy painted across his face. And there it was: his visage drenched, glistening with my essence. My juices cascaded over him, enveloping his lips and even dripping from his nose. I couldn't help but revel in the exhilarating sight before me. The scent and flavour of my wetness were incredibly arousing, enticing every one of my senses. It was a potent cocktail of desire and hopefulness, making me tremble with excitement. The thought of climaxing right then and there crossed my mind, but I resisted the temptation. I craved to prolong this experience, to explore the depths of pleasure he could take me to. With bated breath, I yearned to witness his hunger for me intensify, to discover just how far he would go in fulfilling my deepest secrets.

As I stood in awe of the remarkable sight before me, I glanced over at my boyfriend, who was indulging in his own pleasure. His hand moved up and down his erect shaft, a sinful display of desire. The sight of him only intensified my own arousal, causing me to release passionate moans that filled the room. Sensing my need for a brief respite, I subtly wriggled away, silently requesting a momentary break from the intense stimulation on my sensitive clit. The fear of climaxing into his mouth lingered in the back of my mind, uncertain of how he would react. However, my hesitation did not deter him; he continued his ministrations with unwavering determination.

He gripped my buttocks firmly, pulling me closer to him. With a sudden motion, he flipped me over, my body arching backwards as he spread my cheeks wide open and began pleasuring my tight ass with an intensity that left me gasping for breath. The sound of his lips and tongue working their magic on my sensitive skin echoed through the room, intensifying the sensations coursing through my body. Feeling a surge of desire, I assumed a doggy position, presenting my luscious ass high in the air, craving to be taken from behind. However, I knew this time wouldn't be about penetration; it was about exploring new realms of pleasure. As I tried to remain inconspicuous, a small gasp escaped me, but I quickly buried my face in a pillow to hide any embarrassment. In that moment, his warm and wet tongue glided skillfully over the puckered entrance of my anus before descending down to lavish attention on my yearning vagina. The mixture of sensations sent waves of ecstasy pulsating through every fiber of my being.

I knew he could detect that distinct odor, evidence of my indulgence in a glass of cow's milk, despite my knowledge of being lactose intolerant. Letting out a mixture of pleasure and discomfort, I relished the sensation as his tongue explored every inch of my backside, leaving a trail of saliva in its wake. His persistent moans conveyed an undeniable adoration for rimming, igniting a sense of wonder in my boyfriend, who seemed captivated by the explicit display. Overwhelmed with ecstasy, I couldn't help but release screams of delight as he skilfully devoured my ass, leaving me breathless and yearning for more.

"Baby, oh baby, oh wow, oh dear God, oh Jesus." The intensity of my moaning only increased, driving my boyfriend to the edge.

Unable to resist any longer, he swiftly moved towards us, forcefully flipping me onto my back. With a hungry passion in his eyes, he kissed my lips with an urgency. Without wasting a moment, he began devouring my moist center with an insatiable hunger, his tongue competently exploring every inch. Despite my pleas for him to ease up, the throes of pleasure were overwhelming as I teetered on the brink of climax.

"Cum for me," he demanded eagerly, his voice filled with a primal need. And without any hesitation or restraint, I succumbed to his command and reached the peak of ecstasy.

About ten seconds later, my entire body convulsed with pleasure. It was an intense sensation, unlike anything I had ever experienced before. Waves of ecstasy washed over me as I felt myself squirting and cumming simultaneously. It was a mind-blowing moment that left me breathless and craving for more. In the midst of my euphoria, I noticed that his friend had become eager to join in on the action. With my boyfriend gently laying me down on the bed, I watched as both men hungrily devoured my dripping wet pussy and tight ass. Their tongues danced and explored every inch of my sensitive areas, leaving me writhing in pleasure.

The sight of them competing to consume every drop of my cum took me by surprise. I had never expected my boyfriend, who had never eaten pussy before, to be so enthusiastic about pleasuring me in this way. The intensity of their desire only fuelled my own arousal, making the experience even more exhilarating. In that moment, boundaries blurred and inhibitions vanished as we indulged in our wildest fantasies. It was a passionate and unforgettable encounter that pushed us all to new heights of pleasure.

At this point, I was still experiencing an intense and continuous release of pleasure fluids; it took me an additional six minutes after reaching climax to finally bring my squirting to a halt. As the waves of ecstasy subsided, my body felt utterly drained, leaving me unable to move, speak, or even meet the gaze of the two men who had just brought me to such heights of pleasure. In that vulnerable moment, I slowly shifted my exhausted and shattered form deeper into the comfort of the bed, pulling the soft duvet over me for a sense of solace and protection. Within seconds, I could hear my boyfriend engaging in conversation with his companion, expressing gratitude for their shared experiences and bidding farewell.

I listened intently as he leisurely ignited a cigarette and retrieved a refreshing drink from the refrigerator. With his casual demeanour, he approached me, planting gentle kisses on my cheeks.

In a seductive tone, he whispered, "I adore you, baby."

Overwhelmed by his affectionate words, I found myself speech-less, my body quivering with love. In that moment, it dawned on me that this man was willing to go to any lengths for my pleasure. And ever since that unforgettable experience, no one else has ever matched his expertise in performing oral sex on me. My boyfriend, or rather, my now-fiancé, possesses an extraordinary talent with his lips that has become my ultimate obsession, and yes, he is in fact my fetish.

Until it's my turn I will write
With love,
Chavanese Wint